Barbara was smiling.

All brides should be smiling, even through their tears of joy, so there was nothing remarkable about that. But there was something remarkable about the way she smiled. It was as if she was commanding her lips to part and her white teeth to show, but could not command her eyes. As she drew closer to Rollison, she darted a glance towards the spot where he was standing, and he felt sure that the glance was of fear and not of joy.

He felt a stab

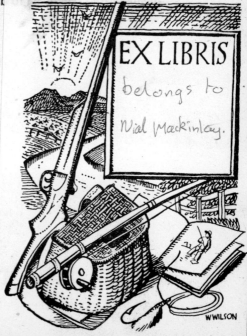

**Also in the same series,
and available in Coronet Books:**

The Toff and the Runaway Bride

John Creasey

CORONET BOOKS
Hodder Fawcett Ltd., London

Copyright © 1959 by the Executors
of John Creasey deceased

First published 1959
by Hodder and Stoughton Ltd
Coronet edition 1963
Second impression 1974

Printed in Great Britain
for Coronet Books, Hodder Paperbacks Ltd.,
St Paul's House, Warwick Lane, London, EC4P 4AH,
by Richard Clay (The Chaucer Press), Ltd.,
Bungay, Suffolk.

ISBN 0 340 18624 0

CONTENTS

1

THE WEDDING

On that beautiful morning in May, the Honourable Richard Rollison certainly lived up to his soubriquet, for he was known as the Toff, and he looked like one. He was resplendent, as a newspaper put it that evening, in morning dress and a magnificent embroidered waistcoat, which had suddenly become *de rigueur*, and in a few months' time would be quite frozen out.

He was not alone, in garb or contentment; there were a hundred and twenty-three other men at the wedding, all dressed as he, except for the waistcoat, which was worn only by the few who contrived to be ahead of fashion. There were also a hundred and ninety-seven women, as well as a sprinkling of adolescents.

According to the society columnist of the same newspaper, it was a most touching wedding. The bride so sweet and young, the groom so proud and manly, the parson, a prelate, gusty rather than prosy, pungent but not long-winded and the soloist among the choir-boys reached a purity of tone which held even hardened sinners spellbound. Rollison was dry-eyed but not unaffected. He knew both bride and groom, and they had his blessing as well as a wedding present of astonishing unoriginality: a clock. True, it was an unusual clock, and they had asked for it, but he was not greatly proud of the gift.

He stood with the hundreds of others in the lofty, lovely church, with many women dabbing at their eyes and some men wishing they could blow their noses, and waited for Barbara Lorne, who had just become Barbara Lessing, and

7

Guy. Guy was a head taller than his bride, and twenty years older; he was forty-three, Guards, broad-shouldered, curiously blond and strikingly handsome; a lion of a man. He stared straight ahead of him, as if on parade, with Barbara's arm resting lightly in his, and two pages dressed in gold and blue holding high her train.

Barbara was smiling.

All brides should be smiling, even through their tears of joy, so there was nothing remarkable about that. But there was something remarkable about the way she smiled. It was as if she was commanding her lips to part and her white teeth to show, but could not command her eyes. As she drew closer to Rollison, she darted a glance towards the spot where he was standing, and he felt sure that the glance was of fear and not of joy.

He felt a stab of alarm and of bewilderment.

Then she was past, and there were undertones of "Isn't she lovely?" "Isn't she radiant?" and "Aren't those pages sweet?" The pages, twins aged seven, seemed likely to be bowed down by the weight of brocade in the pure white train, but they strode on manfully, and the first of five bridesmaids was ready to leap to their rescue if they showed any sign of faltering.

The organ music swelled out, filling the great nave, the bridesmaids passed, each looking more beautiful than she was because of the loveliness of pink and cream. Then came the father of the bride, alone, and the tall and dignified parents of the groom.

The cavalcade passed by, and yet Rollison seemed to see only the fear in the eyes of Barbara Lessing, *née* Lorne. He wondered if anyone else had seen it; and if any had, had simply believed that she was nervous and excited, or else suffering from a natural reaction, poor child, after such excitement. Certainly none of the comments, whispered with proper respect in the church, suggested that anyone but he had been so startled by Barbara's smile.

Then the guests began to file out, with measured tread, into the bright sunlight which bathed the church, the grey brick of nearby buildings, the bright green of the grass in the middle of Parliament Square, the tall tower of Big Ben. Outside were hundreds of sightseers and dozens of policemen and, of course, the Guards, there to do their comrade honour.

And there was an army of photographers.

Until he reached the side door, Rollison moved as lethargically as the rest; once he reached it, he sped outside and pushed his way through the crowd, stepped on to the pavement and hurried towards the front entrance, to appear as one of those who had waited. Barbara was on the steps of the church, and the bridesmaids and the best man were lining up beside her and Guy Lessing.

Had he not hurried, Rollison would not have heard the man who brought sensation here. He was elderly, greyhaired, and had the look of a tramp brushed up for the occasion. His grey beard was freshly combed and his grey moustache swept back from unexpectedly red, wet lips. He carried a banner which was painted in flaming red, saying : THE BLOOD OF THE LAMB WASHES AWAY ALL SIN. He could be seen from the steps of the church, but no one was likely to be able to read that message. There was a lull, when even the traffic seemed to stop for the photographs, the clicking of cameras sounded like a miniature rifle range; and then the grey-bearded man cried out in a voice which boomed as loud as the chimes of Big Ben :

"*. . . know good reason why they should not be joined together in holy matrimony, let him now speak, or else hereafter for ever hold his peace.*"

The words resounded on Rollison's ears, and the ears of the hundreds near him. Some people were shocked and some annoyed and some were obviously angry.

Rollison watched only the bride and groom.

The bride seemed to sway, and the groom put his arm round her, as if he knew the reason; almost as if he feared that these were not the words of a fanatic, but were aimed straight at him and his bride.

"The blood of the Lamb——" began the bearded man, in that magnificent voice.

"That's enough," said a constable, appearing as if from nowhere, and the man of religion broke off at once. "Cut it out, Joe. You don't want to spoil the bride's honeymoon, do you?"

Two or three people tittered; as was inevitable.

The bearded man's eyes blazed.

"Do you deny me my right to spread the gospel? Do you deny me my right——?"

"You've got all your rights," the constable said. He was a young man, and small by London police standards, but obviously he had a wise head and a sufficient good humour. "All the same, if you start spouting any more here you'll have a crowd gathered round, and then you'll be causing a breach of the peace. So let's call it a day, shall we?"

On the church steps, beneath the magnificent arched doorway, another party had gathered, with the bride and groom also in the middle of it. The cameras were still clicking, and ciné cameras were whirring, for the television, for cinema news reels and for home movies. Only the small group near the bearded man, Rollison and the policeman now took any notice of the interruption, and the policeman stood as if twice his size, defying the old man to boom out again.

"A man's got his rights," the bearded man said angrily, but he pitched his voice low, and turned away. Two people raised a mock cheer. He strode off, looking rather like an Old Testament prophet, with his beard framing his face and his mane of grey hair blown by a gentle wind.

"Nice work," Rollison said to the constable, who grinned his thanks. "Do you know Joe well?"

"He's often about," said the policeman.

"Do you know where he sleeps?"

"Croby's, or Old Nick's," said the policeman, and looked at Rollison curiously, as if he could not begin to understand his interest; then recognition dawned in his eyes, and he went on : "It's Mr. Rollison, isn't it?"

"Yes."

"Surprised you don't know Old Joe," said the constable. "He's been about on and off for a long time. Not quite right in the head in some ways, but he's no fool in others. Strong as an ox, too."

"He looked it," said Rollison, and stared after the departing prophet, who was now striding across the road, as if knowing that no giant red bus, no towering lorry, no swerving private car and no midget auto scooter could harm him. He reached the far pavement and turned towards St. James's Park.

"Be at Marble Arch soon," the constable said. "Honour to have met you, sir."

"I hope we're going to meet again," said Rollison, and smiled, and then saw the crowd sway aside as large black cars came smoothly up to the church gates, and there was much throwing of confetti. Rollison was at the back of the crowd now, and could not see the bride clearly; but he did see that Lessing had his arm round her very firmly, as if she was still in need of support.

The next time Rollison saw them was at the reception. He did not know what had happened between the church and the great house in Devon Square, which looked as if the centuries had been turned back, there was such a display of food and of flunkeys. Whatever the cause, Barbara now Lessing had made a remarkable recovery. Her smile and her manner were alike relaxed, and there was colour on her cheeks and a sparkle in her eyes.

"Guy probably gave her a stiff whisky," Rollison mused to himself, and set about smoked salmon but disregarded caviar. There was a great noise of voices, congratulations, the popping of champagne corks and speeches. The best speech came from the bride's father, a plump ball of a man who looked too hot, was smiling as if it was his and not his daughter's wedding, and seemed a joyous little bundle of middle-aged man. When the newly-weds vanished, Rollison felt comfortably replete. He contemplated a fifth glass of champagne thoughtfully, decided that it would put the finishing touch to the occasion and drank it down. A few minutes later he caught a fleeting glimpse of the bride in a powder blue and black check suit, Guy looking most un-Guards-officer-like in beautifully tailored fawn-coloured cloth, bending low as if he hoped to avoid being seen.

It was all most cleverly done.

He was seen, then; and his car was daubed with white-wash and festooned with balloons and old shoes. He escaped with Barbara in a battered London taxi, watched only by two faithfuls; by half-past three not only the deed but also the drink was done.

A blonde rested a hand on Rollison's arm and a bright smile on to his eyes.

"I'm sure they're going to be wonderfully, wonderfully, wonnerfly happy!"

"Of course they are," said Rollison.

The blonde clutched his hand, as if afraid that he was looking for a chance to get away—as in fact he was.

"When are *you* going to marry?" she demanded, and some of the middle-aged people near her were old-fashioned enough to freeze as with horror. But she had not finished yet. "You're the most eligible bachelor in London, and have been for twenty years, but all you ever do is buy your friends wedding presents. Why don't you find a nice girl, and settle down?"

"It's sad," said Rollison, "but there are too many nice girls. Take you, for instance." He slid his arm round her, squeezed, gave her a kiss which so astonished her that she let him go, surrendering to his embrace. Next moment, she was swaying uncertainly on her own two legs and Rollison was out of sight.

"Well!" she said explosively.

Several middle-aged backs were turned on her.

"Beast!" she burst out.

No one appeared to hear.

"*Brute!*" she hated, and stared towards the spot where Rollison might be, but was not.

He was out in the square, walking towards the far corner and not far away, to his own home in Gresham Terrace. He walked at modest pace because it was very warm, and there was no need for haste. He swung his short stick from time to time, as a man without a care. A few people stared at him, which was not unusual. He took no notice of them but looked ahead, undoubtedly very thoughtful. He kept making himself remember the moment when Barbara had glanced at him while in the aisle; kept telling himself that he had made no mistake, she had really been frightened. And he remembered the way she had flinched when the old man had called out, and the way Lessing had helped her into the bridal car.

Gresham Terrace was a street of tall, graceful houses, many rather drab, some newly painted black and white or blue or white, or just plain black or blue. Number 22, where he had a top-floor flat, was about half-way along the street, facing the terrace of houses on the other side and, beyond, the hustle of Piccadilly, which was out of sight but within earshot. He walked up three flights of stairs sedately, quite used to the fact that there was no lift, and as he stepped on to the top landing, the door of his own flat opened.

His man of genius, Jolly, appeared.

That was hardly remarkable. But the expression on Jolly's face, and the way he placed a finger at his lips, abjuring silence, were astonishing, for Jolly did not customarily look perturbed and flushed; nor did his finger usually quiver, as with excitement.

"*Just one moment, sir,*" he whispered, and made as if to step on the landing and close the door behind him. But before he could do either there was a flurry of footsteps, and a girl called out :

"Rolly, is that you?"

In that moment Rollison fully understood why Jolly had been so affected, for the voice was familiar; quite recently he had heard its owner saying, "I will."

2

RUNAWAY BRIDE

BARBARA LESSING, *née* Lorne, appeared behind Jolly, who had accepted defeat with dignity, and stood aside. Barbara was in that blue-and-black check suit, which fitted her perfectly, and she looked a bride enough to fill the heart of any man. Excitement of a kind Rollison could not then understand gave her beauty radiance. Unexpectedly, fear—or what he had thought was fear—had gone.

"Surely I didn't forget," said Rollison, before she could say another word; and he gained a moment's respite, for that bewildered her.

"Forget what?" she demanded.

"I couldn't have," said the Toff, as if to himself, and he stretched out his arms, took her hands, drew her to him and kissed her firmly on the cheek. "Blessings," he said. "Now that the bride's been properly kissed, she may go off with a clear conscience."

"Don't be a fool," Barbara said. "I've come to you for help."

"Guy deserted you already?" asked Rollison, with a lightness he did not feel even remotely.

"No," said Guy Lessing's new wife, "he hasn't deserted me." She was staring straight into Rollison's eyes, and he waited for the sensation which he knew had floored Jolly; but he had won enough time to be prepared for it. "But I've run away from him," finished Barbara. "It was the only thing I could do."

Jolly bowed his head, as if in supplication.

"I will say this for you," conceded Rollison, "you're certainly your father's daughter, he knows his own mind, too.

15

Let's go in and sit down. If there should be a squeak of this
in a newspaper it would be all over town in the morning."
He took her arm and propelled her into the lounge-hall,
with its etchings and its one Picasso, its thick carpet and its
luxurious chairs. Without a pause, he ushered her into the
big room, a living-room-cum-study, in which was his Trophy
Wall—one filled with souvenirs of crimes he had investi-
gated, and of murderers he had helped to put in dock.

Barbara actually stared at this, and then swung round on
him, eyes flashing.

"It *was* the only possible thing. I mean that."

"I could bear you running away from Guy, even though
it was a bit sudden," said Rollison, "but why did you have
to come here?"

"I couldn't think of anyone else who might help," Barbara answered simply.

"Does your father know where you are?"

"Heavens, no! He'd blow his top right off."

Rollison chuckled. "I can believe it. Jolly, some tea,
please. Barbara, before you say another word, you must put
some powder on your nose, I've never seen it so shiny."

"I couldn't help it," Barbara said defensively, and her
gaze roamed, as for a mirror.

"Too bad," Rollison said. "But I can find you some
powder." He took her arm again, and hustled her out by a
different way, into a passage off which several doors led,
and into one of the rooms; a small, well-lit bedroom, where
the dressing-table might have been that of any beauty-
queen. "You'll find everything you want there," he assured
her, and then went out, closed the door firmly and hurried
along the passage and into the kitchen, where Jolly had
already put on the kettle. The kitchen was small, but boasted
a remarkable and lustrous collection of stainless steel, china
and porcelain; the only antiquated thing in it was Jolly.
Jolly was in his sixties, and at times he looked nearer seventy.
His face was criss-crossed with lines, his jowl was flabby and
he had a slight look of the dyspeptic.

"Jolly," said Rollison urgently, "what else has she told you?"

"Nothing at all, sir."

"How long has she been here?"

"About five minutes. She must have left Major Lessing within an hour of departing for the honeymoon."

"Left him standing," Rollison said, and at last he grinned. "I wonder what this is all about? There's a chance that if Major Lessing is in any mood to think, he'll wonder if she's been in touch with me. If he should ring up, she hasn't. Not until we know more about it all."

"Very well, sir."

"And if he calls in person, give me enough warning to spirit Mrs. Lessing out of the living-room."

"I will, sir," promised Jolly.

And he would.

Rollison went back to the spare bedroom, where Barbara was now sitting in front of the dressing-table, face thrust forward, and inspecting herself closely. She glanced up at him, and then back at the mirror; after a moment, she turned to look at him, and ask:

"Is that better?"

"Much."

"Hypocrite, I haven't touched it with powder," Barbara said. "My nose was perfectly all right. If you've telephoned father, I'll never forgive you."

"I haven't telephoned your father."

She caught her breath. "You haven't heard from *Guy*?"

"I told Jolly to give us plenty of warning if either of them came," said Rollison. "You can take it easy for a while."

She jumped up. "Oh, bless you!"

Rollison backed away, hastily.

"I don't want Guy to turn up and find me smeared with his bride's lipstick," he protested, and looked her up and down, then added with a wicked grin: "In fact, I don't

think I want him to turn up at all. This is a bit cramped
as honeymoon quarters, but——"

"Don't be ridiculous," said Barbara. "You'd lock the
door with me inside and stand on guard all night outside,
I know what *you're* like, even if you do keep a spare room
with enough scent and make-up and clothes for a king's
mistress." She shrugged that remark off; and it was obvious
that she had used the past few minutes to compose herself.
"Rolly, I'm sorry I threw myself on your goodwill, but
there's absolutely no one else who could help *and* be reasonable. Dad would just say 'I told you so', but I really can't
believe it. Just at the moment I feel almost cold-blooded,"
she added, and undoubtedly that was true. "I know I'm
soon going to realise what's happened, then I'll collapse like
a punctured balloon; but just at the moment I'm quite all
right."

"Good," said Rollison. "Let's go and have some tea and
you can tell me all about it. You can't have quarrelled
already."

He remembered the expression in her eyes; the fear; and
the way Old Joe had boomed out, so that she could hear.
And when she was sitting in a large armchair in the room,
with the light from the window shining on to her eyes, he
could tell that the fear still lurked there; she simply had it
under control.

"No, we haven't quarrelled," she said. "We had arranged
to change cars at Ealing Common. Guy had another one
waiting there, with our real luggage—the cases we had in
the other car were all empty. I just left him, at Ealing. He
was checking the oil and petrol, just to make sure that no
one had outguessed him. I got out and walked off, and
caught a train—we were only two minutes from the Tube."

"No word of farewell?"

"No."

"And couldn't he see you?"

"No, the bonnet was up, and hid me."

After a decent interval, while Barbara filled in some

of the gaps, Rollison leaned forward in his chair, and asked :

"Why would your father say that he'd told you so?"

"He's opposed the wedding from the very first," explained Barbara.

"He didn't show any opposition today."

"He thought it was too late to do anything," said Barbara, and tears suddenly welled up in her eyes. "As a matter of fact, he's been a pet. When he realised he couldn't stop it, he turned round completely, and there's nothing he didn't do to get us off to a good start." Now, her voice was breaking, tears were spilling down her cheeks, and she was fumbling for a handbag that wasn't there. Rollison handed her his handkerchief, and then saw the door open. He stood up and crossed to Jolly, took the tea-tray from him, and said :

"Don't come in unless I call."

"Very good, sir."

Rollison put the tray down on a small table between the two chairs, and then stood and watched the bride. She was sniffing and dabbing, and he could not see her face clearly. Her fair hair was beautifully dressed, the hand holding the handkerchief was long and slender, tanned slightly brown; and a single solitaire diamond ring blazed by the side of the gold wedding-ring which was so new. He did not speak, but poured out tea, and when he had finished she was holding out her hand for a cup.

"Sugar and milk?"

"Yes, please." She took a little milk and four lumps of sugar; which told a story in itself. She was a little tear-stained and woebegone, but in some ways Rollison preferred this attitude to the curiously stilted calmness she had shown before.

"Rolly," she said, suddenly, "he's married."

The statement came so flatly, that obviously she felt quite sure. Now she looked up into his eyes, cup in one hand, other hand held out towards him, as if for comfort; and he took it. Fresh tears welled up in eyes which were the most beautiful blue.

"At first I couldn't believe it, but now I know it's true," she went on.

Everything Rollison knew of Major Guy Lessing made him want to cry out that he knew her statement was false. Guy was no saint, of course; and any father might understandably try to prevent his daughter from marrying a man years older than herself, and a man often a subject for scandal. Guy's name had been linked with a dozen beautiful women, and there were good reasons to believe that it had not been all rumour. That he would change his mistress almost without regret was common knowledge. That he had married Barbara Lorne for her father's money was common belief, too, except to a few close friends who would not even think of it. But that he should commit bigamy was quite unthinkable.

This was not the moment to argue with his bride.

She had finished dabbing again, and was sipping her tea; Rollison wondered whether she had drunk much champagne, before or after cutting the cake. He remembered the great cake, too, and the hundreds of guests, and the brisk and witty speech of her father.

"What makes you so sure?" he inquired.

"This," Barbara answered simply, and slipped her hand to the V of her coat, delving between the curving beauty of her breasts; and she drew out a most prosaic thing, a folded paper. He had seen paper folded to much the same size, and of the same green print before : this was a marriage certificate. She thrust it towards him.

"While I was getting dressed this morning, someone telephoned and said he was married, and that if I went on with it, she would come to the church and stop the marriage, but—well, nothing happened. I couldn't believe it then," went on Barbara, as Rollison unfolded the certificate, and she watched with a curious kind of fascination. "But during the—the ceremony I hardly heard a word, I don't know how it was I didn't faint. When the bishop asked—asked if anyone knew any reason why we shouldn't be lawfully wedded, I felt as if I would scream. It was *awful*."

It must have been the most dreadful moment of her life; the very moment when she should have known a kind of ecstasy. Studying her face now, Rollison knew how she must have fought for her self-control, and he understood the look in her eyes when she had walked past on her bridegroom's arm. And he could imagine what she had felt when the old tramp had boomed out those particular words for the world to hear.

"*. . . know good reason why they should not be joined together in holy matrimony, let him speak now, or for ever hold his peace.*"

"When we were being photographed, some man shouted out a protest, I don't know whether you heard him," Barbara went on. "I think I would have fainted then, but Guy realised that something was the matter, and held me up. The awful thing was that I could even *begin* to believe it, at first. Then when we got to the reception, there were some letters for me. I found them after I'd changed into my going-away outfit. In one of them was this."

Rollison had the certificate open now, and knew the worst; that this looked real, felt real and said that Guy Lessing, whose profession was given as "retired soldier", and whose address was a friend's country cottage he had used for many years, had married a Helen Goodman, of the village of Bane, where the cottage was; and the record said that the marriage had been solemnised in a North London Registrar's office three years ago.

"I just didn't know what I was doing," Barbara went on. "I couldn't ask him about it, not then, because even if it were true he would deny it, and—well, I didn't know what to do. I stuffed it into my bra, and all the time we were driving to Ealing it seemed to stick into me, like a knife. Then we stopped, and—well, I've told you what I did. I just had to get away, and talk to someone who would try to find out the truth. Rolly, you will, won't you? You'll find out if this is genuine, or if—if it's forged?"

Rollison opened his lips to say, "Of course," but before he uttered even a syllable, the front-door bell rang so fiercely that it seemed as urgent as a fire-alarm.

3

ANXIOUS GROOM

BARBARA was on her feet on the instant, and Rollison felt her fingers clutching his. Jolly, who could have gone through another door, came in this way to show that he was fully alive to the dangers if this should be the groom or the father of the bride. He left the door open wide, so that Rollison could look into the hall, and see whoever had called. Above the lintel of this door was a small mirror which reflected the likeness of anyone standing outside; a recent innovation and a credit to Jolly's inventiveness. Now Jolly glanced up at this, and Rollison felt his own heart pounding.

Jolly, who had made no sound, turned and mouthed:

"*It is Major Lessing.*"

"Who is it?" breathed Barbara.

"It's Guy," said Rollison. "You've got to do a vanishing trick." He took her arm and propelled her across the room and into the spare bedroom. "I'll get rid of him as soon as I can," he promised, "but if he finds out that you're here I don't suppose there's a thing I'll be able to do."

Barbara nodded understanding.

As he closed the door on her, Rollison saw the bright glitter in her eyes, and saw fear fresh upon that brightness. He wished that there had been more opportunity to talk to her, but there was too little time to do what he wanted now, for Jolly would be opening the front door. Rollison went swiftly into the big room, to remove the tea-tray and the evidence that two had been in here; but the tea-tray was not in sight. He grinned as he heard Jolly say:

"Good gracious me!" and saw him back away from the door as if this were the most unbelievable thing that had

23

ever beset him. He actually staggered, and it was the most convincing act.

Rollison put the certificate into his pocket, as Lessing came striding in. He took no more notice of Jolly than he would of a private standing to one side, but approached Rollison vigorously, tall, handsome, obviously deeply perturbed.

"What the devil's the matter with you?" Rollison demanded, and his tone and his expression were at least as convincing as Jolly's. "Why——"

"Have you heard from Barbara?" Lessing demanded.

It would be easy to over-emphasise denial, and Rollison knew that if he did it would do much more harm than good. So he simply raised his hands in resignation, and said:

"No, of course I haven't."

"No 'of course' about it," said Lessing. He came within arm's reach of Rollison, and stood there rather like an accusing Colonel. "This is the most likely place she'd come to, if she were in trouble, and she's in trouble all right."

"Guy, I don't want to appear dumb, but would you mind telling me what all this is about?"

"I'll tell you what it's about," said Lessing, and looked over his shoulder as if to tell Jolly to go out of earshot; but if Jolly were eavesdropping, he was safely out of sight. "She ran away from me." He pressed a strong brown hand against a broad brown forehead, and went on in a harsh, hurt voice, "Give me a whisky and soda, will you?"

"My dear chap!" Rollison hurried to a corner cupboard which contained a remarkable variety of alcoholic liquors, took out a bottle of Scotch and a syphon, half filled a glass and added only a splash of soda. He took it to Lessing. "Plenty more where that came from."

"Thanks." Lessing took a deep drink. "It's unbelievable, isn't it?"

"If I couldn't see you with my own eyes I certainly

wouldn't believe it," Rollison said. "What——" He broke
off. "Take your time, Guy."

"Hardly require any time," said Lessing jerkily. "It's
quite simple. I could see that something was agitating her
at the ceremony and at the reception. I thought she was just
having a reaction. Didn't give it much thought at all, but
coming out of the church, she nearly collapsed. Gave her a
stiffener of brandy in the car going to the reception, and
that seemed to make her feel better. She *said* she was all
right. Afterwards we were to change cars at Ealing
Common, I wanted to make sure that we got away on our
honeymoon without our clothes being full of rice and confetti. Never could stand that kind of asinine child's play.
Then I checked the car levels, to make sure no ass had fooled
around, and—goddammit, she'd walked out on me. I didn't
even see her go."

"She couldn't have been well," said Rollison weakly,
and went to the corner cupboard. "After that, I need
a drink." He poured a weak one, and appeared to toss
it down, then came back. "She must have given some
reason."

"Don't be a dolt. She just walked out on me."

"I could understand it before the wedding——" Rollison
began, and saw the glint spring to Lessing's eyes; for there
was a quarter of Irish ancestry in Guy Lessing, and it was
always liable to spring out to defend the English blood in
him.

"What the hell do you mean by that?"

"Now, Guy——"

"Don't stand there saying 'now, Guy'. What made you
say you could have understood it if she'd left me before
the wedding?"

Rollison gulped. "Her father," he said.

Lessing glowered. "So you know what a fight he's put up
to stop us from marrying."

"He hinted at it."

"Didn't know you knew him well."

"He knew me well enough to know that I knew you," said Rollison cautiously.

"You mean to say that the old so-and-so came to you to check up on me? Why, if I'd known that——"

"He just came for a friendly chat, and you cropped up as if by accident, but I could read between the lines," explained Rollison. "You once told me, standing in this very room, that he would rather cut your throat than let you marry her."

Lessing relaxed.

"Daresay I did," he conceded. "I never liked the bouncy little bounder, how on earth he managed to sire a daughter like Barbara I don't know. But he wouldn't be behind this."

"He wouldn't?"

"It stands to reason. He would hate the scandal—he's the social climber of the century, and he would have given half his fortune for a real live lord as son-in-law. I could believe he'd do anything up to the last week or two, but once he realised that Barbara was adamant, he—but what's the use of standing here and talking about him?"

"Think she'd go straight to him?" asked Rollison.

"No, I don't. But if she was so overwrought that she would walk out on me she might do anything. As a matter of fact, I was prepared to wager that she'd come to you. Sure you haven't seen her?"

"Damn it, Guy——"

"You forget that I've seen you before, and when you play Mr. Innocent you're at your slyest," said Lessing flatly. He downed the rest of his drink. "Wouldn't mind another. I don't mind admitting to you that this has knocked me right over. Still don't really believe it, but . . ."

He went on talking.

Rollison took his time pouring out, and glanced round out of the corner of his eyes. He saw Lessing moving towards the door which led to the rest of the flat, and felt pretty sure what was in the other's mind. Lessing had been coming in and out of this flat for twenty years, and there was little that he did not know. He was much more shrewd than he allowed himself to appear, covering his shrewdness with an excess of old school tie and Guards' affectation. Now he stood as if admiringly in front of the trophy wall, and most would have admired or else been appalled by the choice of lethal weapons.

But Lessing knew each one, and familiarity had bred indifference. He could come into this flat and hardly look at the wall.

Each article which appeared to interest him was a little nearer the door. In a moment or two he would be within a stride of it. Rollison took his drink across, as if casually and without the slightest sign of alarm; he put the drink down and, at the same time, pressed a bell-push under the top of the desk. The buzzer in the kitchen hardly sounded. Lessing edged towards the door, and actually turned round to smile broadly at Rollison in a mechanical way, and to say:

"I've often wished I could take a hammer like that to old Lorne."

"Barbara would never come back to you if you did," said Rollison.

Then Lessing swung round towards the door, and grabbed the handle.

"What——" began Rollison, as if astounded.

The door opened inwards, and banged against Lessing's toe; it seemed as if it also caught him on the nose. He staggered back, while Jolly appeared, looking flummoxed for the second time that day, and covered with embarrassment which seemed quite genuine.

"I am *ex*tremely sorry, sir."

"A'right," mumbled Lessing.

"Guy, what on earth——?" began Rollison, and then broke off, his voice ending on a high note. "Oh, no! You weren't going to see if Barbara was in the flat, were you?" He raised his hands, in a motion of surrender. "I give up. Jolly, take Major Lessing through the flat, room by room, and if he requests it, lift up all the bedspreads so that he can see underneath, and open every wardrobe and cupboard door."

"Very good, sir." Jolly was almost himself again.

Lessing was still covering his nose with his hands, but that was pretence, for his eyes were not watering.

"All very well for you," he mumbled. "Oh, well, I'm sorry. But you must admit that it's the kind of thing you would do."

"The thing I want most is to see the pair of you together again," said Rollison firmly. "I have never subscribed to the theory that you were interested only in the money aspect of this marriage."

Lessing took his hands away, and now looked hotly angry.

"Tell me anyone who did."

"Half the London we know."

"Rolly, are you going out of your way to insult me?"

"I'm going out of my way to make you realise that I don't think you're a cold-blooded fish, and that I don't think you could fail to be in love with Barbara. I've no idea what's wrong, but I'll gladly help to put it right if you think I can."

Lessing said, "There's one thing you can do."

"What's that?"

"Find Barbara for me, and tell her I must see her, and know what it's all about."

"I'll try to find Barbara."

"You'll keep it confidential, won't you?"

"As hush-hush as I can. I could ask the Yard——"

"Keep the Yard out of this, or it'll be all over the newspapers!"

"You mistrust the Back Room Boys," said Rollison, a little sadly. "I can't make any promises, Guy, but I'll gladly do what I can. There's a way you can help, too."

"I don't know a thing."

Rollison asked flatly, "Do you know why she ran away? Have you any idea what drove her to it?"

"I simply haven't the faintest idea," said Lessing, with such quiet emphasis that Rollison felt persuaded that he was telling the truth. "As far as I know, she was hilariously happy about the whole prospect up to yesterday afternoon. I saw her at tea-time. She was overjoyed because Lorne seemed to have come round and was making the best of it, and I don't think she'd ever been happier. I don't think I had been, either," said Lessing, and that seemed to be wrung from him; it was almost touching. "Find her, Rolly, and find out what drove her to do a crazy thing like this."

"I'll try all I know," Rollison promised again.

Then the telephone bell rang, and the tension in the room was so great that the sound made both of them jump. Lessing stared at it. Rollison recovered quickly and went towards the corner of the desk, where the instrument stood. His hand was on the black receiver when Lessing gave his fierce, handsome smile, said, "Sorry about this," and without hesitation, went through the door leading into the rest of the flat.

He would go straight to the spare bedroom.

The telephone bell rang again.

Lessing would find Barbara, and that would be that.

Jolly put his head round the door.

"Will you answer the call, sir, or shall I?" As he finished, he put his finger to his lips again, and actually made a thumbs-up sign.

"Wha'——" began Rollison; then he caught on, gulped, grinned and lifted the telephone. "Richard Rollison speaking," he said, and wondered if by freak of chance this could be Robert Lorne.

He heard the coins drop into a prepayment box, before Barbara said breathlessly :

"Rolly, it's me. Jolly said I'd better go out the back way, and ring you and find out whether to come back, or whether you'd like to meet me somewhere else. I don't want to see Dad, and I'd much rather stay with you, if you don't mind your reputation being at stake."

"Where are you?" Rollison asked.

"At a call box in the Arden Hotel."

"Wait there until Jolly or I come for you," said Rollison, "and while you're waiting, try to recall every word the woman said to you on the telephone, and everyone who could have put that marriage certificate in your changing-room. A list of the names would be a great help."

"Bless you," said Barbara fervently, and added with a catch in her voice: "How is Guy? Does he seem dreadfully upset?"

"Yes."

"Why can't *you* confront him with the certificate, and find out what he says?" asked Barbara. "I've just got to know the truth of it. I'm beginning to hate myself already, but I can't go back to him until I know, can I?"

"You could, but I shouldn't," Rollison said. "Don't go far away, and——"

"Rolly, I must go, a woman I know has just come in," Barbara whispered fiercely. "If this leaks out it'll be a dreadful scandal. *Good-bye*."

She rang off.

And Guy Lessing stepped into the room.

4

GUY LESSING

ROLLISON replaced the receiver on Barbara's last word, and looked across at Lessing; there was a possibility that he had noticed something which might betray the fact that his bride had been here; but a glance into his clear bold eyes, the eyes of a man of great physical courage, told Rollison that all was well there, at all events.

Rollison said mildly, "You might try believing me, Guy."

"Yes. Sorry. But I could have sworn that you're the one person Barbara would come to if she was in any trouble."

"What makes you so sure?"

A smile found its way reluctantly to Lessing's eyes, and curved his thin lips. He had a very square jaw, and rather jutting eyebrows; a Tarzan with all the trappings of London's West End.

"She had an exaggerated sense of your prowess, after the first time I brought her here and she saw those knick-knacks of yours." "Knick-knacks" was heresy where the trophies were concerned, but Rollison did not even flinch. "As a matter of fact, I told her that if I were ever in a jam you were the one man I'd come to for help."

"Are you in a jam now?" asked Rollison mildly.

"You know damned well that I am."

"I don't mean simply because Barbara's run off. I mean, in the reason for her decision to leave you standing."

"Rolly," said Lessing very earnestly, "I haven't the faintest idea why she should run off. I've told you that. I expected to be at a little cottage in the New Forest by now, I've a pony down there as an unexpected wedding present for Barbara. I knew that all the blasted newspapers and

my so-called friends would take it for granted we were
going overseas, so I fooled them by fixing this cottage for a
week, and I've arranged to take a car on to the Continent
next week, for a month's touring. Life was as nearly perfect
as I ever expected it to be. I knew people talked about the
difference in our ages, but I thought that would be accepted.
I can't think of another single reason why Barbara should
get cold feet. The one thing that worries me is that she
looked almost scared at the ceremony. I keep telling myself
it's impossible, and then start wondering if someone had
frightened her away. Once I get to that stage, I boggle,"
confessed Lessing, and threw up his hands. "But what the
hell's the use of talking?"

"This cottage in the New Forest," said Rollison, almost
apologetically. "Where is it?"

"In the village of Bane."

Where a certain Helen Goodman had lived, thought
Rollison reflectively.

"Whose is it?"

"Tony Carruthers. He's out of the country most of the
time, and I've an arrangement by which I pay for the up-
keep any time I go down there. I often use it for week-
ends," Lessing went on, and his jaw seemed to thrust forward. "I know that most people think I slip away for bed-
time orgies to Bane and also to Paris every few weeks, but
as a matter of fact whenever I go away, I go for a rest. In
spite of rumour, I've enough money to live on, and capital
for a farm when Barbara and I have decided where to settle.
We're not sure it'll be England. Anyway, the first time I
went to Bane was after that scandal—you know. I had to
get away from gawping crowds and society columnists, and
went down to the village for three weeks. Did me a world
of good. Bit of riding, fishing, walking. But what has that
to do with the present situation?"

"Did Barbara know you were going to start the honeymoon at Bane?"

"Good lord, no!"

"All a secret operation," murmured Rollison, and wondered whether Lessing proposed to plan his married life as a military manœuvre, and what Barbara would think if he did.

"I wanted to surprise Barbara," Lessing added tersely.

"Well, she certainly surprised you. Guy, what are you going to do while you're waiting? You're not one of the world's patient souls."

"Damned if I know what to do," growled Lessing. "I take it for granted that Barbara's in London, but there's no reason why I should. I suppose, as she hasn't been here, the most likely place for her to go is her father's, but I hate the thought of going and telling him. If he doesn't know already, then he'll bounce for joy when he hears."

"He's not such a bounder."

"You've never been his prospective son-in-law." Lessing tossed down the rest of his whisky-and-soda; he seemed incapable of sipping it, and every movement and every word was jerky. "What do you suggest that I do?"

"Go down to Bane."

"*What?*"

"It's a two-hour run. You can drive hell-for-leather and when you get there you can unpack and get everything ready. If I find Barbara, and everything's all right, I can bring her down, or telephone you to come and fetch her."

"Cottage isn't on the telephone," Lessing said, but his eyes were kindling. "Might be a good idea, though. You could telephone a message to the pub, the Old Rufus. I certainly can't just stand around here and do nothing. Think I ought to see Lorne first?"

"No. I'll find out if Barbara's gone home."

"I don't want his suspicions aroused, if she hasn't. If he thought that she had walked out on me he'd laugh his head off. Then he'd start worrying about the scandal."

"Guy, go down to Bane," urged Rollison. "Telephone here two or three times *en route*, Jolly or I will be waiting with a message. If there's no answer you'll know we haven't had any luck."

"That's what I'll do," decided Lessing brusquely. "Rolly, find her for me."

Rollison didn't speak.

"If anything's happened to her, I——" began Lessing, and then he broke off, seemed to grit his teeth, and moved towards the door. "Thanks. Sorry I mistrusted you. It's Rufus Cottage, Bane. See you soon."

He was so anxious to be on the move that he was outside before Rollison could get to the door and open it. He went down the stairs at the double, heels clicking, and Rollison felt quite sure that he had sustained the worst possible blow to his pride. If this story reached the newspapers he would be driven almost to a point of desperation, for he would feel that the world was laughing at him, and would hate the sound of mocking laughter.

Rollison closed the door.

Jolly appeared.

"Jolly," said Rollison on the instant, "nip round to the Arden Hotel, and find Mrs. Lessing. She was by the telephone boxes. You know the main foyer, don't you? There are plenty of odd corners, and she'll be sitting in one of them, out of sight. Take the car, get her inside it so that no one has a chance to recognise her, and then drive her to Lady Gloria's."

"Very good, sir," said Jolly.

"Now."

Jolly moved almost as swiftly as Rollison could, and a minute later he went out with a bowler hat placed firmly on his head and a stride nearly as brisk as that of Lessing. Rollison waited until his footsteps had faded, then went to the window. Lessing was not in sight; he felt reasonably sure that Lessing now trusted him.

Rollison took the marriage certificate out of his pocket, and read it again. There was everything, black on green and white. Here was the evidence of the marriage of Major Guy Lessing to Helen Goodman, spinster.

Rollison took out a road atlas of Southern England,

studied it, found Bane, and looked up the village in a gazetteer; there was a population of one hundred and ninety-three. Among them, presumably, was Helen Lessing, *née* Goodman. He found himself looking into space and seeing Guy's face when he had suggested that he should go down to Bane. Guy had not hesitated for a moment; and it was impossible to believe that he would knowingly take Barbara to that village for their honeymoon.

"It simply doesn't make sense," Rollison said aloud, as he sat at his desk, picked up the telephone and dialled the number of a doctor who lived half a mile away; at one time an Army doctor, also in the Guards. He listened to the ringing sound, until a woman answered.

"Is Dr. Willard there?"

"Who wants him, please?"

"Richard Rollison."

"Oh, hallo, Rolly," said Doc Willard's wife. "You aren't going to keep him for long, are you? He's got a night off."

"Ten minutes," promised Rollison.

"*David!*" Mrs. Willard called, into the distance, and then came back to Rollison. "Rolly, have you ever known a wedding go more smoothly?"

"Never," answered Rollison firmly.

"Dave was saying that he thought Guy must have planned the operation months ahead, and rehearsed it for weeks. Not that you could rehearse a man like Bobby Lorne! Wasn't he good?"

"Very good."

"And I thought Barbara looked——" began Mrs. Willard, and then broke off. "Here's Dave."

"Hallo, Rolly," said David Willard, in a voice both deep and resonant; the kind of voice which was likely to make a man move the receiver inches from his ear. "Been eating too much, or did the champagne upset you?"

"All bubbly does is make me babble," said Rollison, and went on in exactly the same light-hearted tone: "Don't let

Alice know that I'm going to ask about Guy Lessing, pretend it's about the Charity Ball Committee."

Willard played up perfectly.

"Yes, old chap?"

"I know I'm being mysterious, but you'll have to wait until I can see you for an explanation," said Rollison. "Guy was wounded in Egypt, wasn't he?"

"Yes."

"Head wound?"

"Yes."

"Any possibility that it would result in black-outs or temporary amnesia?"

"Well, I don't know," said Willard, and obviously he was taking time to collect his thoughts. "It was a nasty wound, he's lucky to be alive. Kerrington did the op." Obviously his wife was no longer within earshot. "I wouldn't say I expected trouble, but it could happen. Why?"

"He seems to have forgotten something he did three years ago."

"Hm, yes," said Willard. "That was a few months after the operation. Could be. How serious is this?"

"Serious enough to ask you to check with Kerrington but not urgent enough to want immediate action," Rollison told him. "Can you let me know what Kerrington thinks, some time in the morning?"

"Yes. No trouble in the love nest, is there?"

Rollison found himself grinning. "Not yet," he said. "Thanks, Dave, give Alice a wonderful night out."

He rang off, swinging his leg. The obvious explanation of part of the mystery was that Lessing had married this Helen Goodman while suffering from amnesia. It would not satisfy many people unless there was the nearest thing to positive proof; and at this distance from the marriage, proof would be impossible to find. But medical reports might be enough to satisfy Barbara, and even her father. And probably it would make sure that the little matter of bigamy was only a technical one.

He would bring Lessing back, on some pretext, when he made his first telephone call, and go down to Bane himself. He wanted to see this Helen Goodman, or at least find out if she still lived there. She might point a finger at whoever had sent that marriage certificate and had made that telephone call.

Barbara had said that a woman had spoken to her.

Helen Goodman herself?

If so, why hadn't she interrupted at the ceremony? Had she been in the church, but lacked the courage to stand up and cry: "I forbid this marriage"? Such timidity was possible, but it did nothing to explain the bearded Joe and his booming voice, heralding doom and declaiming that one particular sentence.

Rollison heard footsteps on the stairs.

He took it for granted that this was Jolly, back with Barbara; they had been quick, but neither of them would have wasted time. The question was: what should he say to Barbara? Should he talk of this head wound and the possibility of amnesia, or should he wait until he knew more?

The footsteps sounded on the landing.

He realised then that they were not Jolly's, and in fact there had been hardly time for Jolly to collect Barbara, take her to Lady Gloria's Marigold Club and then come on here. A moment later, the front-door bell rang; and Jolly would not be without a key. Rollison went to the lounge-hall, thinking only that he must get rid of him quickly, and glancing up at Jolly's mirror.

Robert Lorne, the father of the bride, was outside.

5

FATHER OF THE BRIDE

IT was not difficult for Rollison to look surprised, and he had time to notice that Lorne's round, usually red face was pale, and that his eyes, usually so merry, were grave. He was an ebullient man, both mentally and physically, and that was the chief reason for the fact that he and Guy Lessing did not get on well together; Lorne was the antithesis of everything that Lessing believed a man should be, for Lessing was a conventionalist in nearly all things.

"Good lord!" exclaimed Rollison. "Come in." He stood aside and closed the door. "What's on your mind, you look as if you've buried Barbara, not wedded her."

"That's how I feel," said Lorne. He was a head shorter than Rollison, and had to hold his head back to look into Rollison's eyes. "I knew all the time that Barbara was making the mistake of her life. I didn't trust Lessing, and my God, I was right. Did you know he was married already?"

Rollison was already on the move, towards the big room, the trophy wall, and a respite.

"Come in," he said, and by the time they were in the big room, his expression showed only bewilderment. "I take it you're serious."

"Of course I'm serious. Do you think I'd joke about a think like that?"

"I don't get it," said Rollison.

"You could answer my question."

"I can't answer it, because I don't believe Guy was married."

"You will," said Lorne, and put a plump, pink hand to

38

his coat pocket. He wore a pale grey suit, beautifully tailored, and a dark grey tie. His dark hair shone, his cheeks shone, his manicured nails shone and his black shoes had a sheen of remarkable brilliance. He took out a folded paper, which looked identical with the one which Barbara had given to Rollison. "Here's a copy of the marriage certificate."

"Good lord!"

"Nice friends you have," Lorne said bitterly. He was deeply hurt and desperately worried for his daughter, and in that moment looked almost pathetic. "Rolly, I don't know what to do. Read that for yourself, you'll see there's no mistake. I wish to heaven I'd checked more closely, but would anyone believe a thing like this was even possible? I knew that he was a womaniser, but——" Lorne almost choked.

Rollison studied the certificate, although there was no need, for he knew every word, and every name. This looked as if it had been copied by the same copy-plate hand-writer, and it was also like a sentence of doom for Guy and Barbara.

"Satisfied?" demanded Lorne.

"No. I simply can't believe it."

"Oh, be yourself," snapped Lorne. "It's no use being a sentimental fool even if the man was a friend of yours. I hope you won't try to defend him." His lips were twisted, and that pain showed in his eyes. "Believe it or not, this isn't the main thing I've come to see you about," he went on, and took the certificate back. "I want some help and advice. Are you free to help me?"

"Yes."

"And you won't allow your friendship with Lessing to bias you?"

"No."

"Well, then, here's the problem," said Lorne, and he moved towards the window, as if he could not bear to meet Rollison's eyes any longer. "An hour ago, I had a telephone message from someone in the London area. It was a woman. She told me that this earlier marriage had taken place, and incidentally that it had been consummated over a long period. She said that she would release the story and a copy of the certificate to the newspapers unless I was prepared to pay ten thousand pounds to keep it quiet."

Rollison didn't speak, but watched the back of the plump man's head. There was a hint of a bald patch, which looked very white.

Lorne spun round.

"Well? Struck dumb?"

"Bob, you won't help Barbara or yourself by losing your temper," Rollison said mildly. "What came first? The telephone call or the certificate?"

"The call." Lorne hesitated. "At least, I think it did. The certificate was brought up to my study by the footman, with the evening newspapers." Lorne talked very flatly, and mostly out of character; it was as if everything except his portly little body had been deflated. "That's the kind of inquiry you handle, isn't it? Blackmail."

"I'll handle this one. Where were you told to hand over the money?"

"I am to post ten lots of one thousand pounds each to ten different addresses, all in the Greater London area," answered Lorne. "Here is the letter of instructions. You'll see that I've been given until tomorrow afternoon to get the money, parcel it up and send it. There's a different name at each address." Lorne gave a tired little smile. "I'm glad that you're as shaken as I am. Whatever else, we have to admit that it is remarkably well organised."

"We certainly do," agreed Rollison, and took the letter. It was on flimsy paper, and the note as well as the names and addresses were all typewritten. No address was given at the head of the paper, and there was no signature. There was a kind of cold efficiency about it which told of a detached and dispassionate mind.

"What do you advise?" asked Lorne bleakly. "Shall I

pay and keep them quiet until I've had time to warn Barbara? That's the hell of it—that poor Barbara is going to get a shock like this. You don't——" He gulped, as if he hated what he was about to say. "You don't know where they're going on honeymoon, do you?" He hardly paused. "No, of course you don't. Lessing didn't even tell Barbara, it was all to be such a great surprise for her. I'd give my right hand to stop her from spending the night with him, and I mean that. My first reaction was to telephone Scotland Yard and ask them to stop them, wherever they are, but I realised that they've probably flown abroad, and that I can't stop them anyhow. Once the Yard had it, the whole thing would leak out."

"The police can keep a secret," Rollison said.

He could take the father of the bride into his confidence, and lift a tremendous burden off Lorne's shoulders; but if Lorne knew the truth he would almost certainly want to see Barbara, would tell her about Lessing, and would then refuse to pay the money, telling the blackmailers to sing for their money. Rollison felt quite sure of that. As a consequence, Guy Lessing would be damned, for now and for a long time to come.

Lorne would know, sooner or later, that his daughter's marriage had not been consummated.

"Well, what shall I do? Pay up?" Lorne demanded abruptly.

"I think I'd take a chance and pay one, not ten, thousand pounds," reasoned Rollison, very thoughtfully. "One hundred in each packet instead of one thousand." He saw the interest that suggestion sparked in Lorne's blue eyes. "That will keep them on a piece of string. They'll argue that as you've paid something, you'll divvy up the rest under pressure. And you'll have gained a little time for me to work in."

"I'll do that." Lorne was brisk. "Good idea." He was more relaxed than he had been since he had arrived, and he moved to a chair and sat down. "All I want is to find Barbara, so that I can tell her myself. We'll face it together, after that. I'll hate the scandal, of course, and so will she, but better to see it through and be done with it. Don't you agree?"

"Yes."

"What do you think is the best chance of finding them quickly?"

"Calling in the Yard."

"It's the last thing I want," said Lorne grimly. "You know them pretty well over there, don't you?" He glanced at the trophy wall. "I remember the Home Secretary once told me that you were a much better detective than the newspapers gave you credit for. The newspapers put it all down to glamour and personality, but apparently the Criminal Investigation Department concedes that you're a rival. I'd much rather you handled this yourself, Rolly."

It would help to say that he would.

"I'll certainly try," said Rollison. "How about a drink?"

"Not on top of that champagne," said Lorne. "I'd have the world's worst headache in the morning, and I never needed a clearer mind. Rolly, what about your fee? Name your own."

"Forget it."

"That I won't."

"If you feel stubborn when it's over, haggle with Jolly," said Rollison, "but this is one of the jobs I'd rather do for love than money. Bob, you never trusted Lessing: why?"

Lorne answered without a moment's hesitation.

"His reputation with women, plus his blasted air of superiority. He seemed to think that Eton, Sandhurst and the Guards turned him into a little tin god. He hasn't a penny to bless himself with, either. The only thing I had to say for him was that he seemed genuinely in love with Barbara, but after this—I could choke the life out of him with my own hands."

"Bob," advised Rollison firmly, "don't even try. Don't do a thing on your own. If Lessing could play a trick like this, then there's some quality in him I didn't know about, and he's capable of doing anything. Don't get involved any farther than you are. Leave it to me. In the long run that will be a lot better for Barbara and much better for you."

"I suppose you're right," conceded Lorne, and gave a tight-lipped smile. "He'd probably break me into little pieces, anyhow. When will you start work?"

"The moment you've gone."

"I'm on my way," said Lorne, and seemed to bound to his feet. "Let me know the moment you've news, won't you? And if you can get hold of Barbara tonight——"

He broke off.

"If it's possible I will," Rollison assured him, and went with him to the door. "I'll have this list of names and addresses copied, and send one to you in the morning."

"I'll get the money," said Lorne grimly. "You notice that they stipulated used pound notes. Who'd you think is behind it? The real wife?"

"It's too early to start guessing," Rollison said evasively.

"Yes. I'll see myself out," added Lorne. "You get busy, minutes might make a difference in this."

Lessing had reached the door ahead of Rollison, and now Lorne did so, too, but that was because Rollison made it easy. He heard the latch click, and Lorne pulled the door wide open. They heard footsteps.

Jolly's? wondered Rollison.

Jolly had been a long time, Rollison realised; he had been so anxious that his man should not come back with his story until Lorne had finished that he had forgotten how long; perhaps it had taken longer than he had expected.

This was Jolly . . .

The moment he set eyes on him, Rollison knew that all was not well, that Jolly was a worried man. Sight of Lorne startled him, and he drew to one side, said, "Good evening, sir," and when Lorne nodded, turned away quickly.

"Good night, Rollison, and thanks," said Lorne, and went

bouncing down the stairs, while Rollison waited for Jolly, alarmed by his man's mood.

"Mrs. Lessing wasn't at the hotel, sir," Jolly reported. "I've been to every room on the ground floor, everywhere. She simply isn't there."

6

HIGH SPEED

THAT was where the bottom dropped out of the affair.

While Rollison knew where Barbara was, the situation was under control. Now it was out of hand. He was already engaged on three fronts: for Barbara, for Guy, for Lorne.

He owed Guy loyalty and the benefit of the doubt, if nothing else. Probably the best thing to do now was to tell him the truth, and make him explain, if there was anything to explain.

There was the problem of the blackmailer, and the problem of this Helen, *née* Goodman, who might be the blackmailer's aide.

"Jolly," he said, "I'm going to drive down to Bane. When Major Lessing telephones, ask him to meet me at Rufus Cottage."

"Very good, sir."

"Wait for an hour, and if Mrs. Lessing hasn't telephoned, have a word with Superintendent Grice, at his home if necessary. Tell him from me that there's urgent need to find Mrs. Lessing, and could he help—keeping it as quiet as possible."

"Very good, sir." Jolly had fallen back to his impassive norm.

"And find out from Mr. Grice what he knows about a hot-gospelling sandwich-board man by the name of Holy Joe."

Jolly did not turn a hair.

"I will see to it, sir."

"Thanks," said Rollison.

He was glad to get out of the flat, and was actually sitting in the car, which Jolly had parked outside, when he realised that he was still in morning-dress. He grinned as he started off. For the first twenty minutes, the traffic gave him plenty to think about, but after that he was able to travel without much difficulty, and soon he was on the open road. It was not yet six o'clock, so he should be at the cottage about eight. Once he was on the Great West Road he let the car show what it could do, and out-paced everything going his way. He enjoyed driving; the car seemed almost like a well-trained animal, and for the first time since he had reached Gresham Terrace, he could let his thoughts drift. The obvious answer to the mystery was that Helen Goodman and an associate were blackmailing Lorne, but did that square with the threat to Barbara? Wouldn't it have paid the blackmailer better to have worked on Lorne alone? How could anyone be sure that Barbara would not confide in her father immediately?

There was another odd thing.

Someone had threatened to intervene during the ceremony; and someone had been carefully prepared to try to extort money from Lorne—extortion which would be quite impossible had the wedding been stopped.

"Which doesn't add up, unless two parties are involved," Rollison said musingly, and then spent ten minutes chasing a Bristol whose driver seemed to think that nothing on the road could catch him up.

In five minutes under two hours, Rollison was turning into the lane which led to Rufus Cottage.

This was on the Romsey side of the forest, on its very fringe. The village of Bane was in open land, where cattle grazed, but just beyond it the great oak and beech and birch trees of the forest grew stately and massive, and the road to the cottage led between these trees along a track which was little used. It was not buried deep, and was only five minutes from the main road. Rollison caught a glimpse of thatch through the trees; and the sun was striking the thatch and the west corner of the cottage, and shining on flowers and lawns which proved that a gardener laboured greatly here.

Rollison had expected to see Guy Lessing's car; but there was no car.

No one was in sight, but a brown pony grazed in a tiny paddock. The honeymoon gift?

Rollison drew up on a patch of green just outside the cottage, which was in a clearing, with the nearest trees a hundred yards away. A few shaggier ponies were grazing on open land, but no one was in sight : a large *Trespassers Will Be Prosecuted* probably kept picnickers away.

It was very warm, and he felt a little ridiculous in his morning-dress, but did not think much about it. He wondered uneasily why Guy hadn't arrived. He had had a long start, and should have made his first telephone call from Staines or somewhere near—in fact, Rollison had expected the call before he had left. Nothing was straightforward, and it looked as if he was going to miss the chance of telling Guy what had caused the trouble.

He wondered if Barbara had turned up yet.

Barbara missing; Guy missing. Was there any connection between those two facts? Was it possible that Barbara had gone to a hiding-place which Lessing had known about —and had he gone there on the off chance of finding her?

A church clock struck eight.

Rollison opened the gate of the cottage garden, and then saw the square Norman tower of the church, between the trees; he had not seen it from the straggling village itself. In the distance there was a hum of cars; here there was only the hum of insects.

Rollison reached the front door and lifted the iron knocker. The door was of solid oak, gnarled, cracked and knotted, and obviously centuries old; so were other dark oaken beams in the walls. Age seemed to be standing beneath his hand as he banged. There was no response, but the door yielded an inch or two. He pushed and it opened wide.

He stepped inside.

Until that moment he accepted the possibility that Guy was in the cottage but hadn't heard him come; also the possibility that the car itself was parked somewhere out of sight. He bent his head as he crossed the low-ceilinged room, which had some old pieces of furniture and a smell of furniture polish, but was not as picturesque as the outside promised. He went through a doorway and saw a flight of twisting stairs. That was when he heard a faint sound.

He stood at the foot of the stairs.

"You there, Guy?"

He could not be sure that the sound had been the movement of a man or woman, and he did not hear it again; and there was no response. He glanced along the narrow passage towards the kitchen, and then towards the stairs. As the stairs were nearer he actually started up.

Then he saw the hand on the floor.

He had not been able to see it at the foot of the stairs themselves, but from the third tread the angle was different, and he saw it. It was a woman's hand, quite shapely, and it lay limp upon the stone slab. The position was so odd that it shot alarm through Rollison. He turned awkwardly on the narrow space, then strode towards the kitchen; he forgot to duck, and banged his head on a lintel which was no more than five feet nine from the ground.

He fell back, head ringing, eyes smarting, and the pale hand seemed to be going round and round; but that was illusion, it was there on the floor. He pushed the door a little wider, and stepped into the tiny kitchen, with its small windows, the big dresser along one side, the open hearth with an electric cooker and a refrigerator standing side by side and looking incongruously clean and white.

Behind the door, curled up, one arm flung about her head, the other pressed into her bosom, was a young woman in a bright-blue frock.

At one glance, Rollison was afraid that she was dead.

He stood for a moment, staring at her, prepared for the

shock by what he had already seen, and yet hating to admit the inescapable. She lay so still. Her hands were so shapely but work-stained and red. He could see one ear, pink and pretty, poking out from hair so dark that it was almost black, so curly that he felt sure that the curls were natural. He could see another thing, the wicked thing: a cord tied and twisted tight round her neck.

The momentary paralysis lifted.

Rollison stepped across the outstretched body, went down on one knee and moved the woman. The knot was buried in a neck which had been smooth and white. Her mouth was slack, and he could just see the white of the teeth. Her eyes were partly open.

Her hand was warm.

He felt no fluttering at the pulse, but there was a chance to save her, and only he could do it, for ten minutes might make the difference between life and death. He took his penknife and began to cut the cord with desperate urgency. It meant that he had to cut her flesh, too, and there was a little blood. He had to use the blade as a saw, once it was underneath the cord.

He thought, "Not Guy."

He had sent Guy here.

The cord parted, but it was so deeply embedded that it did not fall away; that was the moment when he felt sure that there was no hope. Whoever had killed this woman had meant to make sure there was no chance that she would come round. But Rollison had to try artificial respiration; and he had to send for help.

He turned the woman over gently, on her front, with her head turned to one side. Once he started he mustn't stop, and if he wasted seconds now, seeing if anyone was outside, he might throw away what chance he had. So he knelt down, and began to apply the pressure. His back was to the window and the back door, and he could see the foot of the stairs. He heard no sound. He kept telling himself that this could not have been done by Guy Lessing, but he could not convince himself. A new kind of dread entered his mind: that this was Helen *née* Goodman; that this was Lessing's wife.

To and fro, to and fro; weight on, off; on off; on off. Slowly, steadily, without any pause, that was the way : to give the lungs every chance of drawing in air again. He knew at heart that there wasn't really a chance.

He could not get Guy out of his mind. He could not believe it of the groom, but—well, the car wasn't here, yet he had come down here.

But he had not planned to, as far as Rollison knew; that was a point to remember : he had sent Guy here, so nothing could have been premeditated, unless . . .

Had this woman been waiting for him, expecting to confront him and his "new bride"?

If she had——

Rollison heard a sound behind him, a slight slithering, and for the first time since he had started the artificial respiration he stopped and twisted round; but all he saw was an uplifted arm, a gloved hand and a weapon in it; a hammer. He flung his own arms up, to protect himself. He felt the full force of the hammer on his right wrist, and the pain was so great that he cried out. He pitched forward, sprawling over the woman, but kept his arm over his head, knowing that there would be another attack, and fearful of what would happen if this assailant struck and struck and struck again. He felt a glancing blow on the side of the head, and tears of pain blinded him; then he received a savage blow at the nape of the neck and lost consciousness.

His last thought was fear of death.

. . . . .

He remembered that when he came round. There was darkness and a humming noise which he knew was inside his head, and then flickering light which hurt his eyes and grew brighter. The humming sound was louder, as if an aeroplane was flying overhead; and swooping lower and lower, as if to crash. The light was blinding. He moved his head, and winced; he moved his left wrist, and pain streaked through it.

He realised that he was still on the floor.

He rolled over and saw the woman, just as he had left her; limp and lifeless. He got to his knees, slowly. It would be impossible to try to help her again, but that didn't matter; it was impossible to help the dead. He tried to get to his feet, but his legs wouldn't carry him, and the humming had become a pounding in his head. There was a table near him. He edged towards this and pulled against it with his right hand and then hauled himself to his feet. He swayed. He ran his right hand over his head, gingerly; there was a smarting wound on top, from the first blow, and that was bleeding a little; but the nape of his neck was much more painful. He couldn't turn his head without pain.

Then he heard voices.

He thought that they were excited, a man's and a woman's, but he could not be sure. He heard a flurry of footsteps, like distant thunder, and every footstep seemed to send more pain through his head.

Then he heard footsteps inside the cottage. He stood facing the open kitchen-door as an elderly man came in, breathless, and a younger one followed; the younger one carried a pitchfork, and the glint in his eyes suggested that he longed for a chance to use it.

They saw him.

They saw the woman on the floor.

The older man, small, compact, dressed in old tweeds, as obviously from the country as the trees outside, drew in a sharp breath, and said, "Don't move."

The younger man did not speak, but stared at the woman, and then moved towards her, fearfully, still gripping the pitchfork. His eyes were no longer bright, but anguished, and suddenly he let the pitchfork go, and flung himself on his knees beside the woman.

"Helen," he gasped. "Oh, Helen, speak to me."

7

POOR HELEN

"Helen," the young man sobbed.

"Don't move," the older man ordered.

"I've got to sit down," Rollison said, very carefully, and he moved towards a Windsor chair standing close to the table, and lowered himself. "What——" It was even an effort to speak. "What brought you?"

"Never mind what brought us, we're here."

"If you get a doctor instead of standing there, you might have a chance to save her," Rollison said to try to break the impasse, and each word sent pain shooting through his head.

The man seemed startled, as if that was a new thought. "Aye," he said, and looked down at the youth, who was holding the girl's right hand and pressing it to his lips; as distraught as a man could be.

"Go and get a doctor," Rollison said. "Can't you see that I'm in no shape to move?"

"Arthur," said the older man, so sharply that he made the other look up. "Watch un. I'm going for Dr. Brasher, I know he's home, I saw him half an hour ago. Watch un, now."

"I'll watch un," Arthur muttered.

There was no hope for the woman Helen—who could it be but Helen *née* Goodman?—but at least the tension was broken. As the old man went out, there came a new tension, for Arthur bent down and picked up the pitchfork, holding it in his hands as if it were a pike. He stared at Rollison with a single-minded hatred which could not be misunderstood. There was no point in arguing, point only in making sure that if he did lunge, the gleaming prongs could be thrust aside. Rollison sat quite still, prepared to throw himself to the right or left, while the older man went hurrying outside, footsteps sharp on a concrete yard, and then muffled by turf or soil.

The old man shouted to someone.

The tears glistening in the young man's eyes were tears of grief, now, and the hatred seemed to be dimmed, although the weapon was still held forward, as if it would be thrust into Rollison's chest if he so much as moved.

Rollison broke a silence which seemed to have lasted for an age.

"Will he bring the police as well?"

"Just sit still," the young man ordered.

"The quicker the police come——"

"The quicker they'll put you in prison."

"Why don't you use your head?" asked Rollison testily; and his own head hurt abominably with the effort of speaking. "She was dead when I arrived. I tried to save her life."

"You're trying to talk your way out of it, more like. Don't you move."

There was a curious kind of lilt to the man's voice; it was like that of a radio actor using a dialect. But there was no doubting his intention to stand guard as a bulldog; nor doubt of his grief.

The two men came hurrying back, and Rollison knew that he need not keep up this tension any longer. Arthur actually lowered the pitchfork as the old man and another, younger, came in. The newcomer was not the doctor. He was massive and burly, and he looked like a policeman out of uniform.

"Here's the man," the older man said.

Blessedly, the massive man had a quiet voice, a calm expression and goodwill.

"You look as if you've had a nasty time, sir," he said, and went straight to the girl. "Who gave her artificial respiration?"

The two men who had first arrived looked startled.

"I did," said Rollison.

"I could see from the way she was lying that someone had," said the massive man, and he knelt astride and began to do exactly what Rollison had done, although he must have known that there was no hope. Rollison watched him; the rhythmic movement had a kind of mesmeric effect. Then a car arrived, a man came hurrying, this time an elderly, broad-shouldered doctor, swinging a black bag. He was remarkably brisk, but it was ten minutes before he turned to Rollison, took one look at his head, shook two white tablets on to the palm of his hand and said :

"Take these. Arthur, get a glass of water, please, for this gentleman. Blake, you'd better telephone to Winchester, hadn't you? You've a case of murder on your hands."

. . . . .

The tablets did not work miracles, but after ten minutes of pounding, Rollison's head began to feel less painful, although he could not turn it with any comfort. The doctor had a look at the cut on the back, declared that it was nothing to worry about, dabbed it with antiseptic and declined to put on a plaster.

"You don't want a bald patch there," he said. He had taken control completely now that the massive Blake, the local police-constable, then off duty, had gone to summon the Winchester police and so hand this over to the Criminal Investigation Department. The woman's body hadn't been moved, but was now covered with a sheet. Arthur stood by the window, clenching and unclenching his hands, while the older man, grey, hardy, berry-brown, watched Rollison with a curious intensity. There were a dozen questions in Rollison's mind, but the urgent one was screaming.

Had Guy Lessing been here?

He had been using a hired or a borrowed car, and Rollison did not know what make it was.

He knew so little.

Arthur and the older man, his father, had been coming

to the cottage, where the father was the gardener and general handyman when anyone was in residence. They had seen a man running away, had known that Helen was here, had come running and been shocked to a point of horror at what they had found.

Helen *who*?

Rollison still wasn't sure. He was almost sure, but could not believe that coincidence would stretch so far, so—Helen *who*?

The father and son were vague about the man running away, for the old man's eyes were not good, and the young one had been behind him. They had known that Major Lessing was coming down here, had been asked to make special preparations, including dinner for tonight.

Helen had been preparing that.

It wasn't making any sense.

One thing was obvious, although no one had said a word: that Arthur had been in love with the dead Helen, and would readily kill her murderer; he was not yet convinced that the murderer was not Rollison.

Then a car arrived, an ambulance immediately after it, and there was an invasion of plain-clothes men with cameras, equipment, finger-print powder. All the routine of a murder investigation began, and the man who questioned Rollison was Chief Inspector Wilfred Reno, whom the Toff had met several times before.

.   .   .   .   .

There were times when the only possible thing was to tell the police the whole truth.

This was one of them.

Reno asked questions, made notes, sent messages to Winchester, made it clear that he expected his superiors to consult Scotland Yard at once, and then said almost casually to Rollison :

"Yes, the dead woman's name was Goodman before she got married. She was a very quiet type. Her parents died

years ago, and everyone thought she would marry Arthur
Lloyd." Arthur was now outside, nursing his grief if not
his pitchfork. "She went off one week-end and came back
with a wedding-ring, but she wouldn't give anyone any
details, except that she'd married a gentleman—she probably meant officer and gentleman," Reno added, with heavy
sarcasm. "She went off every now and again, after that,
sometimes for a week-end or two, sometimes for a week or
more. When she's at Bane she lives alone in a tiny cottage,
and does housework and cooking for some of the people in
the bigger houses near by."

"An officer and gentleman," Rollison echoed. "No
name?"

"She said her name was Smith," Reno told him, and this
time kept a straight face. "That was her way of telling the
village that it was her business and she was going to keep
it so. She was a strong-willed young woman, and had her
way. We'll soon find out whether in fact she married Lessing."

"Do you know where she was married?" asked Rollison.

"I believe the only man in her confidence was the Vicar
of Bane, and he's on a church outing. He should be back
by ten o'clock."

Rollison glanced at his watch; and pain streaked through
his neck.

It was a little after nine.

"Meanwhile, there's a call out for Lessing, on the strength
of what you've told us," Reno went on, "and the Yard say
they're looking for Miss Lorne or Mrs. Lessing. Know what
I'd do, if I were you?"

"You'd take a room at a local hotel, get the doctor to
give me a sleeping-draught, and sleep solidly for eight
hours," said Rollison, "Then you'd feel better in the
morning."

"That's it!"

"What I'm going to do is wait until you've had word
from London about the register, and then get someone to

drive me back to town," Rollison said. "That's unless you
tell me I mustn't leave the vicinity."

"Oh, you can go as far as London," Reno conceded
airily. "I don't mean you're clear of suspicion, of course,
but you'll be all right in London, the Yard will watch you!"

"Thanks very much," said Rollison dryly. "I'd like to
telephone my man. Any objection to that?"

"None at all. Stroll as far as the village, that won't hurt
you," Reno said.

In fact, the cool night air did Rollison good. It was still
daylight, although dusk was dimming the brightness of the
sky. Already dozens of people were standing about and
watching the cottage, and others were streaming from the
main London-to-Bournemouth Road. Some children were
admiring the pony. A dozen cars were in sight. Six policemen had been drafted in, to make sure that no one went
too close to the cottage, and Rollison realised that everyone
was watching him. A slender young man wearing a big
lumber jacket of bright tartan, a jersey cap and a pair of
loose-fitting grey flannels showed especial interest.

He was standing close to the path which led to the village.
The motor road was in the other direction. Ahead was the
church and several cottages, one of them marked Post
Office; the telephone would be outside that. Rollison went
on, and glanced again at the youth in the bright tartan;
then he realised who it was.

He stopped.

He knew that Reno had sent a plain-clothes man after
him, ostensibly to see that he was all right, so he did not
speak to the "youth", who was in fact Barbara Lorne.

.   .   .   .   .

"No, sir," said Jolly. "Mrs. Lessing did not get in touch
with us again. I am extremely sorry that I was not able to
find her."

"Forget it. How about Major Lessing?"

"He has not called, sir."

"In short, an absolute blank," said Rollison gloomily. "Right, Jolly, I'll be back by midnight, all being well."

"Are you sure you wouldn't be well advised to stay in Winchester until you've had a chance to recover from the attack, sir?"

Rollison hesitated.

"I could be at the end of a telephone all the time," Jolly urged.

"Do you know, I believe I will," decided Rollison, and he kicked open the kiosk door so that the constable and the bride-in-pants could hear. "I'll stay at the Roebuck Hotel in Winchester, if there's room."

"I think that's very wise, sir," approved Jolly.

Rollison rang off, went past the policeman and saw Barbara moving towards the telephone. He took no further notice of her, but walked back to the cottage, already feeling much better than when he had left, yet even more puzzled. If Barbara had not wanted to be recognised she would not have come so near, but—how was it she had come here at all? Had Lessing told her about the cottage for the first part of the honeymoon?

If so, why had Lessing lied to him about that?

Rollison reached the cottage and saw that two men in overalls were running a telephone cable from the village to the cottage; that would be for the police. He also saw Reno standing big and burly over a slim, very youthful parson, who carried a heavy walking-stick. The parson looked distressed, but Rollison could hardly wait for him to go away and for Reno to approach him.

"Yes. They were married in Hampstead," announced Reno. "The vicar once took the trouble to go and make sure, and saw the entry. Major Guy Lessing, soldier, retired, bachelor, was married to Helen Goodman, spinster, of this parish."

If the name Lessing meant anything to him, he concealed it well.

8

SUSPECT

RENO used his influence, and a room with bathroom attached was available for Rollison at the Roebuck, a hotel of distinction on the outskirts of Winchester. Reno, apparently determined to be friendly, drove Rollison in the Rolls-Bentley; on his own admission, it was the first Rolls car he had driven in his life. It seemed to purr past the double-decker bus just outside Winchester, and certainly he did not notice the tartan-clad "youth" who was sitting in the bus and looking down on the magnificent car.

It was half-past ten, the bar was closing and most of the customers were coming out.

"I'll garage the car," promised Reno, "and I'll leave the key with the night porter. You'll be crazy if you don't go straight to bed."

"I will. Can you use your influence again and have some sandwiches sent up? A lot of sandwiches. I'm famished."

"You're getting better." Reno laughed, and left Rollison at the entrance to the hotel. On each side were round pillars, just inside was a bear rug on dark oak boards, and a tiger skin lay, mouth gaping and teeth bared, in a small smoking-room. There was an air of old-fashioned comfort about the dark brown, the red velvet curtains, red mohair chairs and gleaming glasses.

The night porter gladly offered to bring sandwiches.

"Two, sir, or three?"

"Could you make it half a dozen?"

"Really hungry, sir, are you? I'll fix it. Beer?"

"I hate to say it, but milk. A lot of milk."

"Quite all right, sir, after a bang on the head like you've had. Honour to have you with us, sir."

So the news was all over the town.

Rollison held his head very erect as he signed the register in bold characters which an illiterate could read, and held his whole body erect as he walked slowly up the two half flights of twisting stairs. They reminded him of the stairs at Rufus Cottage; many things reminded him of the cottage, including a picture of some New Forest ponies on the staircase wall. He saw a chambermaid, elderly, grey, tired, smiling, opening a door on the right.

"It is Mr. Rollison, sir, isn't it?"

"Yes, thanks. Ah, room twelve." It was a monster of a room, with a two-poster bed, a head canopy of puce-coloured velvet, a vast oak wardrobe, a creaking floor, oak beams and the bathroom so modern that it seemed to have jumped three centuries. The bed was turned down, the maid left him, hurrying, and he sat gingerly on an upright William and Mary slung chair, to give his head a chance to recover; but although it ached, it was no longer pounding. He heard two lots of footsteps, and then a timid tap at the door. He got up, and opened the door a crack.

"Oh, Rolly," said Barbara.

He stood aside, and she slipped into the room and stood behind the door. She had made a remarkably good job of being a youth, and had even managed to look flat-breasted. But she was flushed now, and obviously scared. Rollison did not help her out, and she said hesitantly:

"I couldn't have made a worse mess, could I?"

"No. How did you know where to come?"

"I remembered the address of the cottage," said Barbara unhappily. "It was rather a silly thing, really. About three months ago, Guy had been caught out in the rain and had to send his coat to be dried, and some letters fell out of his pocket. I remembered it—you know how little things stick in the memory sometimes, and this name was so unusual." She was quiet for a moment. Then: "Rufus

Cottage, Bane. And after I'd seen you this afternoon, I remembered it again."

"Ah," said Rollison owlishly.

"Rolly, why are you behaving like a disapproving uncle?"

"I'll tell you in a minute, when I know whether you realise what you've done." He felt terribly sorry for her; yet in his mind there was a suspicion which he knew would be in the minds of any others when they realised that she had been near the cottage; that *she* could have killed Lessing's real wife.

Impossible?

"Well, it was just after I telephoned you," Barbara explained. "I saw a woman I know socially, an absolute scandalmonger, and I went hot and cold all over. Then I realised that I couldn't go on like that, being terrified all the time in case I was seen, and—well, I suddenly had an overpowering desire to see if Guy was at the cottage. I knew he probably wouldn't be, but I just couldn't help it," she went on, a note of defiance now strong in her voice. "I suddenly felt that I had to confront Guy with it, that it was beastly and cowardly to leave it to someone else. I hated what I'd done, and I felt—well, can't you understand?"

"I might," said Rollison, "if I believed it."

Anger flashed into her eyes.

"Are you saying that I'm *lying*?"

"I'm saying that you haven't convinced me that you're telling the truth," answered Rollison. "Do you know what happened at the cottage?"

"A woman was murdered."

"Do you know what woman?"

Barbara closed her eyes, as if it had suddenly become impossible to keep them open, and she didn't answer; in the quiet, Rollison heard footsteps on the stairs, and guessed what they heralded.

"Helen Goodman," Barbara whispered.

"Helen who used to be Goodman," Rollison confirmed,

and there was no gentleness in his voice, because he wanted to spark a reaction from this unhappy girl. He failed utterly; she simply looked despairing.

The footsteps were nearing the head of the stairs now, and Rollison went on, "The porter's bringing my supper, pop into the bathroom for a minute."

She made no answer, but turned and walked across the creaking boards, past the big bed, through the tall door. She closed it behind her, looking very small and pathetic. Then there came a heavy bang on the door, and a moment later it swung open. The night porter came in with a laden tray on one hand, held high and balanced as if skilfully.

"Here we are, sir," he said brightly. "I think you'll find enough here to look after the inner man." He looked round, espied a small table, then slipped on polished boards and swayed. The tray tilted to an alarming angle. Rollison felt himself leap to save it, and pain shot through his head. The porter weaved and spun his arms and finally brought the tray to an even keel on both hands. With great care he stepped to the table, and lowered his burden almost stealthily. "That was a near thing," he observed. "Nearly upset the apple-cart. You want to be careful, that floor's very slippery."

"I'll be careful," promised Rollison.

The porter stood back and rubbed his hands.

"Well, sir, how's it look?"

It was a feast. Thin slices of bread and thick ham and beef; some firm tomatoes; a huge piece of Cheddar which looked as if it would have a perfect flavour; a tin of biscuits, a slab of butter, and two jugs of milk, glass, knife, fork, everything.

"Wonderful," said Rollison fervently.

"If you get outside of that lot you'll have nightmares, my wife wouldn't sleep with me after it," the porter declared. "Don't worry about the tray, the maid'll see to that in the morning. Anything else?"

"Just tell me where my car key is."

"Hanging up on the hook where the door key is, at the desk. I meant to bring it up, an' clean forgot."

"The morning will do," said Rollison, and half a crown changed hands; Rollison half expected the porter to spit on it for luck, but he did not. "Good night."

"Good night, sir. Sleep tight!" The porter chuckled deeply as he went out.

Rollison waited for the door to close, then went across and turned the key in the lock. When he looked round, Barbara was coming from the bathroom. She had taken off her cap, shaken her lovely hair loose and run a comb through it; she was a girl again. She was troubled, anxious and hungry; and she eyed the tray almost unbelievingly.

"Hungry?" asked Rollison.

"Ravenous! I haven't had a morsel to eat since breakfast, except a piece of the cake." She looked suddenly forlorn. "I suppose I oughtn't to say so, but it gave me awful indigestion."

"Come and sit down and tuck in," Rollison invited, no longer stern; for there was a limit to what this girl could stand, whatever her folly, if folly there was. She came quickly, and her eyes actually lit up; that was the moment when Rollison realised how very young she was, younger in some ways than her twenty-three years.

She bit deep into a sandwich.

So did Rollison, who had not eaten since the wedding breakfast, and then had not eaten much. For nearly ten minutes they concentrated on the sandwiches and the cheese, which did not disappoint. They had two glasses of milk each, too. It was Rollison who finished first; he watched Barbara pick up a few crumbs of cheese on the tips of her fingers and lick the cheese off.

"Locust," he said.

"You were nearly as bad."

"I'm a grown man."

"Yes." She looked at him in a way he didn't quite understand. "This is absolutely ludicrous, isn't it?"

"Not quite the wedding night you expected."

Tears touched her eyes again.

"It doesn't seem as if it's really happening, it's like a nightmare. Rolly, do you think Guy——" She couldn't finish.

"Killed this Helen?"

"Oh, it's hateful even to think it!"

"Apparently you thought it."

"It *isn't* possible, is it?"

"It doesn't seem possible to me," replied Rollison, with great deliberation, "but a lot of queer things have happened, this is the most topsy-turvy case I've ever been involved in. If it weren't for dead Helen it would be the slapstick of the year. How long had you been at the cottage?"

"Only about ten minutes. I got a train to Winchester, and then a taxi."

"What train?" Rollison asked quickly.

She didn't answer.

"What train?" Rollison insisted.

"Well, quite an early one, if I'd come straight from Winchester to the cottage I would have been there long before you, but I couldn't go as I was, obviously. I *couldn't* go in my going-away dress, at—well, could I?"

Was she just being guileless?

"I went to a Marks & Spencers and bought these clothes," Barbara went on, "and I bought a carrier bag to put the other clothes in. I hurried back to the station to change in the cloakroom, and left the bag there. But I know what you're thinking. I could have gone out to the cottage and arrived long before you."

"Yes," Rollison said.

"Rolly, you don't *seriously* think that I could have done a dreadful thing like that?"

"I seriously think that you might be what is called an accessory after the fact; or even before the fact."

"You mean——" She was husky-voiced.

"I mean, if Guy killed her and you knew."

She was absolutely without colour now, and her eyes were feverishly bright.

"I don't believe he could have done such a thing."

"Did you see him at the cottage?"

"No."

"Have you seen him at all?"

"No!"

"Have you seen his hired car?"

"No, I haven't. Rolly, if I had, I'd tell you." Barbara leaned back in her chair, hands on the arms, and closed her eyes; a trick she had which was probably habit. When she opened her eyes again they were unbelievably bright and starry. "Rolly, the thing that frightens me is this : if Guy didn't, who did? Who would want to?"

"That's what we're going to find out," Rollison said. "If I'd reached the cottage half an hour earlier, I would have saved her life."

"What did happen to you?" inquired Barbara.

"I was trying to bring the woman round, and someone clouted me," Rollison answered. "A man who'd been hiding upstairs, and probably crept down, went out the front way, and came in at the back. Didn't make a sound." He was thinking over everything that had happened, feeling the moment of alarm all over again, seeing that clenched hand, that clenched *gloved* hand, with the hammer in it. He remembered the first agonising pain; his wrist was swollen and he could not move the fingers easily; he would not be able to for days.

A hand with a dark-brown leather glove on it; he saw that vividly in his mind's eye.

But there were hundreds of thousands of pairs of gloves like those.

Barbara was closing her eyes again, and this time it was easy to believe that she was simply tired; and that her eyes and head were aching. But she began to speak while he watched her; and he understood only too clearly how it was that Guy Lessing, who was about the same age as he,

should fall in love with her. She was quite beautiful. Even
in this hideous garb, she was——

Desirable.

"The thing that frightens me is that Guy always had these
headaches," she was saying. "He said they started after he
was wounded. When he had one he hardly knew what he
was doing."

She opened her eyes wide.

She had cause to be frightened.

"Barbara," Rollison said, quite crisply, "the doctor gave
me some tablets to make sure of a good night's sleep. I've
enough and to spare. Have you a room here?"

"No, they're full up."

"You take the bed, I'll take two chairs——"

"You won't do anything of the kind," said Barbara, with
a flash of spirit. "You look as if you'll crack up if you don't
have a good night's rest, and this is a beautifully comfortable chair. But I wouldn't mind the tablets, I'd like to get
to sleep. I'd feel better if I could forget everything for a
while."

There was very little to do, for neither of them had night
things or anything for their toilet. Barbara loosened the
waistband of the grey flannels and kicked off her shoes, a
pair of brown slip-ins. Rollison turned off the light and
cautiously eased himself out of his coat, took off his collar
and tie, and loosened everything that needed loosening,
then stretched out on the big, comfortable bed. He could
hear Barbara's even breathing, and did not know whether
she was asleep or feigning sleep. He was still not sure what
to make of her story. The simple thing and the thing he
wanted to do was to believe that it was absolutely true. It
would be easy to understand her sudden change of mood,
her desperate desire to see if Guy had gone to the cottage,
but would she even think of that possibility? Wouldn't she
assume that he would stay in London and look for her?

Had she told the real reason for her visit to Rufus
Cottage?

She turned over in the chair, and her breathing was very soft and even. A young and lovely girl, sleeping, was a few feet away from Rollison. This should have been her wedding night; this *was* her wedding night. There was no doubt about it, but for the murder of the woman named Helen, who had married Guy Lessing, this would have been a bedroom farce.

Gradually, he became drowsy.

Why wasn't it *his* wedding night?

That would be the thing : there was the girl who had asked him point blank why he had never married. Now he was asking himself. Absurd, lazy, pleasantly sensual thoughts drifted in and out of his mind. Man and woman were made to sleep together, not within a few feet of each other. *Was* she asleep? Why couldn't he get to sleep? Had the doctor given him tablets that weren't powerful enough? He was more wide awake than ever he had been, but at least the tablets had helped him; his head was no longer aching. It was crystal clear, except that he could not force himself to think of the problem, only of the irony of this situation. He hitched himself up a little on his pillow, and could just make out Barbara's face in the soft moonlight that was coming in at the open window. Even the moon was merged with his mood.

Moon—mood.

Moon—madness.

Did Guy suffer from a kind of moon madness?

Rollison felt himself much drowsier than he had realised, slid down in the bed again, turned cautiously to one side, and felt himself dropping off to sleep. The drug had taken a hold on him after all, there was nothing he need worry about. Forget Guy, forget Barbara, forget absurd thoughts and ludicrous longing.

He heard a sound.

It reminded him of the one he had heard at the cottage, but that was probably imagination. Perhaps Barbara wasn't asleep after all. She must have turned round in the chair again, cat-like. She was curled up there, wasn't she, like a cat?

Rollison heard the sound again, and it did not come from the chair, it came from outside. He was half asleep, and yet wakeful, telling himself that hotels were always full of noises which no one could understand.

He heard a sharper sound.

In the silence which followed he could hear the soft breathing of the girl.

He began to sit up, very slowly, staring at the window; and as he did so a hand appeared at the window, a dark shape in the moonlight. Then another hand appeared, and a moment later, a man's head and shoulders.

Very cautiously, Rollison lay back, his heart thumping but his breathing steady. He had no weapon handy; if this were to be an attack, he would have to rely on his one good hand.

9

SHOCK

THE window was opening wider as Rollison stared towards it. It was the swing type, and he heard faint noises as the bar which held it steady was lifted off its hook; then the window was thrust wide open, with hardly a sound. It was impossible to see who was there, for the moon was behind the man, whose head and shoulders were in black silhouette, but his hair was fair.

Then a beam of light shot out.

It struck the foot of the bed first, and gave Rollison time to close his eyes by the time it reached his face. He felt the brightness, like a kind of heat, and hoped that his eyelids were not fluttering. He was already planning what he would do when the man approached the bed.

The light was steady on his face, and then a man whispered :

"*Rolly.*"

Rollison kept his eyes closed, but his heart began to pound more violently than ever. That fair hair and that whispered voice were unmistakable when judged together.

"*Rolly!*"

This was Guy Lessing.

He did not call out again, but the torch went out, and presumably he put it in his pocket. He was within two yards of his bride, but she was in a corner, and unless he looked away from Rollison, he would not see her. She seemed to be fast asleep; motionless.

Lessing hoisted himself up on a ladder that was resting against the wall, and began to climb in. It wasn't easy for a big man, but soon he would be right inside the room.

Rollison almost lost the power of thought, but it came flooding back. He must speak to Lessing before Lessing saw Barbara. If he saw her first——

The position of his body made him turn towards her.

"*Who's that?*" Rollison hissed. "Stay where you are!" He sat up in bed as if stung, and Lessing twisted his neck round to look at him. "*Stay there.*"

"It's me, Guy," whispered Lessing.

"Don't move until I put some light on."

"You can recognise my voice, can't you?" Lessing had managed to get one leg in, and now drew the other after him; he had not yet seen Barbara. He stood by the window, staring at Rollison. "If you've got a gun, put it away."

"It *is* you," Rollison gasped, to hold Guy's attention fast.

"Listen, Rolly, I've got to talk to you. Keep your voice low, in case we're heard. No need to put on a light." Lessing was pleading as he came towards the bed, and now he could not see Barbara unless he turned right round. "A dreadful thing's happened. I'm wanted on suspicion of murder."

"So you realise it," said Rollison. He spoke in a whisper as low as Lessing's, and hitched himself farther up in bed, without moving for the light; it was surprising how bright the moonlight was now. But in a moment, any moment, Lessing was certain to hear the other breathing, would turn round, and——

"I've never needed your advice so much," Lessing said. "Ought I to give myself up, or ought I to stay on the run and look for Barbara?"

He could break in here and within a minute of waking Rollison, throw such a question at him. Obviously there was no other thought on his mind; it was obsessional.

"I just don't know what to do," he went on. "And don't tell me that's because there's nothing in army regulations about it."

He was close to the bed.

"Guy," said Rollison, still very softly, "why did you

marry Helen Goodman, and then bigamously marry Barbara Lorne? What kind of madness is this?"

Lessing breathed, "*What?*"

"You heard me."

"You must be mad," said Lessing, but there was a lack of power in his voice, and he caught his breath on the last word.

"If anyone's mad, you are. What on earth made you think you could get away with it?"

"But it isn't true," Lessing replied, and although there was more vigour in his voice, it still lacked conviction; almost as if he wasn't really sure himself.

"In the pocket of my coat, hanging on the hanger behind the door, there is a copy of the marriage certificate," Rollison said.

He was wide awake now, but it seemed as if the drug had taken deep hold of Barbara. He could not understand how it was that Lessing did not notice her steady breathing; it seemed very loud to him. But Lessing stood rooted to the spot at the side of the bed, staring now at the dark shape of the coat behind the door.

"It isn't possible," he whispered.

"Don't be a ruddy fool. Either you married Helen Goodman or you didn't."

"It isn't possible," Lessing said, and his voice suddenly became weak, and he gave Rollison the impression that he wanted to sit down. He put a hand to his forehead, and moved forward a pace. "Tell me you're fooling."

"The police have a copy of the certificate, too. Helen Goodman was killed tonight, a little while before you were due to come to the cottage with your new wife. Explain it all away. I'm listening."

Lessing dropped to the side of the bed.

"My God," he breathed. "Did Barbara find this out?"

"Someone telephoned her before the ceremony, and left her a copy of the certificate after it."

Lessing drew his hand over his forehead, very slowly.

Rollison thought that his hand was trembling; and Rollison felt alarm and anxiety even deeper than he had before. It was a long time before Lessing spoke again, and in the silence, Barbara actually shifted her position, and her chair creaked. Lessing took no notice.

"It's hideous," he said at last. "Absolutely hideous. I suppose I must——"

His voice tailed off.

Rollison knew what he was going to say: that he must have married Helen Goodman during a spell of temporary amnesia. But for two things, that might have been the only necessary explanation. The two things were the demands for money and the murder of the woman. Even the demands on Lorne's pocket would fit in; if someone had known of this marriage, had seen it as a source of blackmail, and decided to act. It was even possible that Helen *née* Goodman had been to the church——

No, that wasn't feasible.

Whoever had telephoned Barbara would not have calmly returned to the cottage and set about preparing for the honeymooners; there were limits to fantasy.

"Hideous," Lessing said, rather more firmly. "No one will believe me, of course, including you."

"What won't we believe?"

"Rolly, listen to me." Lessing leaned forward and shot out a hand, gripped Rollison's forearm and sent pain through the injured wrist; the fingers gripped tightly, angrily. "You've got to listen to me. If I married that girl I knew nothing about it. I wasn't aware of what I was doing. For years I've had black-outs, and when I've come out of them I just haven't known a thing. I didn't realise that anything like this could happen, but it's the only possible explanation. I wasn't aware of what I was doing."

"Presumably you weren't aware of killing Helen tonight."

Lessing's voice rose, as if he had completely forgotten

the possibility of being overheard. The grip on Rollison's arm was almost savage.

"I didn't kill her, I tell you."

"Not even in a black-out?"

"I didn't black out tonight."

"You didn't telephone my flat, either."

"I tried to, from Staines, but the line was engaged, and I simply couldn't stand around waiting. I had to *do* something. I got back into the car and hit the miles so fast it wasn't worth stopping again. Then I saw Barbara in Winchester."

"*What?*"

"I was driving, and saw her walking along the street; I couldn't believe my eyes," said Lessing, as if still amazed. "There was a string of traffic, and I couldn't stop. I yelled out of the window, but some damned great lorry was passing, and I don't suppose she heard. When I did manage to stop and get out, she'd gone. I walked the streets for her, looked in at every café and hotel, I nearly went mad trying to find her."

"Mad enough to black out?"

"*I tell you I didn't black out.*" Now Lessing had lost all restraint, and was shouting. "I went out near the cottage, hoping she'd be there, and there were some police and obviously a lot of trouble about. I wasn't seen, and decided I'd be better off back in Winchester. I hardly knew what I was doing then, everything had gone completely out of control. I was frantic. I had to know what had happened, so I telephoned a newspaperman I know in London. He told me that there was a call out for me in connection with this Helen Smith's murder."

"Did you know Helen Goodman—or Smith?"

"Of course I did. She was daily woman and cook whenever I came down here. My God, Rolly, I was here two or three times a year, she couldn't have been more respectful, it was always Major this and sir that. I didn't give my real name when I went down there—at first I used the cottage to dodge newspapermen, and I called myself Brown. But Brown, Smith or Lessing, if I'd married her she wouldn't have behaved so meekly. She was one of the friendliest souls imaginable, the equable, sunny type. It's utterly unthinkable that we were married; that certificate must be a fake."

That was when Barbara said, "Thank God for that."

10

BRIDE AND GROOM

LESSING turned his head very slowly, as if he could not believe that he had heard aright. Barbara was sitting up in the big armchair, her legs still on an upright one in front of her. Her face was ghostly pale in the moonlight. Lessing stood up. Barbara was staring at him, as if she wanted to examine every feature on his face, to see the expression in his eyes. Rollison had the strangest feeling; that in this moment each had forgotten that he existed.

Lessing moved towards his bride.

Barbara pushed the coat she used as a blanket, and began to get up.

It was like watching a scene played in slow motion, and now Rollison was quite sure that they were oblivious of him. He watched, unable to make himself look away.

With a sudden movement Lessing reached Barbara, drew her up and stared into her eyes; so she was hidden from Rollison. Then they were in each other's arms, half laughing, half crying; and it was almost a sacrilege that he should be a witness to this fierce re-awakening of their love. And in that moment Rollison became quite certain that Lessing had no thought of Barbara's money or his past; this was an instance of two people being absolutely in love with each other.

After a few moments, Rollison leaned over and switched on the bedside light. It was bright compared with the earlier darkness, and Lessing started, Barbara gave a sharp exclamation. Then they separated and turned round, but their arms were intertwined as they stared at Rollison.

"I'd forgotten you," Lessing said, and gave a short laugh.

"There's something else you don't believe." When Rollison didn't answer, he went on, "I don't know whether I ought to thank you for looking after Barbara or break your neck for being in her room."

"It's his room," Barbara told him.

"He could have left it to you," said Lessing, but he was jesting in a grim way. His eyes widened. "Could he, though? You look as if a ton weight's fallen on you. Who hit you, Rolly?"

"Whoever killed Helen Smith-Goodman."

"Ah," said Lessing, and his arm tightened round Barbara. "Back to reality. Well, there isn't much more I can say—did you hear everything, Bar?"

"Everything that mattered, I think," answered Barbara, her voice quite steady. "You said that if you married this Helen you weren't aware of it, and that you certainly didn't have a black-out tonight, and didn't kill her. All that matters is that I believe both, darling, and I do."

"It might be quite important to persuade the police," Rollison interpolated.

"They'd never seriously believe that if I knew this servant and I were married, I'd bring my bigamous bride down to the cottage!"

"Queer things happen, and you might have paid Helen to keep quiet. Wives have condoned bigamy before."

"Don't be a lunatic."

"You should read the *News of the World*," Rollison said mildly. "The police would be prepared to believe that you came to an arrangement with Helen, that she decided not to keep it, and you killed her."

Neither Lessing nor Barbara spoke; both looked shocked.

"The fact that Guy came down to the cottage regularly and that Helen looked after it for him makes that theory look more than possible," Rollison said. "It could be very impressive circumstantial evidence, with Helen not here to give evidence for the defence. The fact that he used a false name looks odd, too. There may have been a good reason for that, but will it be easy to make it look reasonable to a jury? False names hide a multitude of sins. Guy, you're in a bad spot."

"Do you have to gloom like this?" Lessing demanded, and it seemed as if the presence of Barbara had given him back all his confidence. "Don't you believe in 'truth will out' and that kind of thing? And haven't I briefed the best detective in the country to find out the truth?"

"Guy," said Rollison soberly, "there's really only one line to follow which would help." He looked at Barbara. "Your father was approached today and told that unless he paid over a large sum of money, the story of Guy's alleged earlier marriage would be given to the newspapers." He ignored the gasp which exploded from Barbara, and the exclamation which Lessing stifled, and went on, "That's the line I shall follow, but you and your father are going to have to accept one thing."

"What is that?" demanded Lessing.

"The whole story will have to come out."

After a moment :

"We can't help that," said Barbara practically.

"Yes, I suppose it will," agreed Lessing, and added almost wearily : "If it were simply the matter of this previous marriage, we'd face it, but with a murder added——" He broke off, and there was a long pause before he went on, "I suppose the police might stretch it even farther and say that Barbara was in the know all the time."

"They could."

"Rolly, what can you do?" asked Barbara, her voice now soft and scared.

"We need a lot more time to think this out," answered Rollison, and changed the subject without warning. "How did you know I was here, Guy?"

"I saw the hotel register."

"When did you come in?"

"I was still hunting for Barbara," Lessing told him. "I thought she might have given a false name, but I was bound to recognise her handwriting, so I made a trip of all hotels. You'd just signed in when I came here. There was an old salt of a porter on duty, who said there wasn't a room left for the night, but if I was really stranded I could sleep in the lounge. He sits so close to the foot of the stairs I didn't have a chance to come up this way, but I know the hotel fairly well, and was pretty sure that your room was this one, or next door. So I went out the back way. There's a court-yard, ladders, everything I needed to come up and see. I was scared stiff in case I opened the window of the wrong room, but——" He broke off, and gave an unexpected grin. "Isn't it time you did some explaining, too?"

"Barbara will explain everything that's necessary," Rollison told him, and got off the bed cautiously. "I think I'd rather be in London than in Winchester in the morning, and I don't know that there's any need for me to go to the cottage again. Guy—these black-outs."

"They're genuine."

"I know they are!" Barbara broke in. "They must be."

"How long do they last?" Rollison asked.

"Usually only an hour or so."

"What's the most likely thing : that you went through this ceremony with Helen Goodman during a black-out, or——"

"When you first put it to me, I almost believed it was possible," said Guy Lessing quietly, "but now that I've had time to think about it, I know it wasn't. There would be the licence to get and all the plans to make, it couldn't be done in an hour or two." He gulped. "I don't believe I'm a schizophrenic case. That's the only rational explanation now, and I just don't think that it's true."

But he could not be absolutely sure.

"It's ludicrous even to think of it," Barbara said, as if that settled the whole question.

"What *is* the best thing to do?" asked Lessing, trying to be rational. "Give myself up to the police, I suppose, and let them work out what really happened."

"It might be," conceded Rollison, "but I'm not sure yet. There's one little matter the pair of you may not have realised. That if you didn't marry Helen Goodman, someone did—and in your name. And he persuaded Helen to say she married a Smith—and so make sure that it looked as if you were anxious to be anonymous."

"Good God!" exclaimed Lessing.

"Of course!" cried Barbara, eyes blazing with new hope. "All we've got to do is find out who it was!"

"That's all," agreed Rollison dryly. He slid his feet into his shoes, then put his right foot up on a chair and tried to tie the laces with one hand. He couldn't manage it; suddenly Barbara came across and tied the laces for him. "Thanks," he said, and whispered : "*Want me to go?*"

She looked into his face while she was still bending over his shoes. Lessing may have heard, but Rollison was not sure. Barbara looked so very young and lovely, and her eyes were quite radiant in her love. She formed one word but did not utter it :

"*Please.*"

"What's this muttering?" demanded Lessing.

"Guy," said Rollison, standing up, "you're a lucky man. I'm supposed to be in this room, and no one will be surprised if I'm still asleep at nine or ten o'clock. Don't leave unless you're forced to. I'll call you as early as I can."

After a long pause, Guy Lessing said hoarsely, "Well, you couldn't tell us that you're on our side more plainly than that. Thanks. But are you well enough to leave?"

"I wouldn't like to trust myself on that ladder, you'd better shift it, if you get a chance. I'm well enough to get out downstairs without the porter or the police seeing me —if the police have taken the trouble to leave a man around, which I doubt—and drive to London," Rollison said. "I've a duplicate key of my car." He shrugged himself into his coat, gingerly, and grinned. "Believe it or not, I've been to a wedding."

He blew a kiss to Barbara, and unbolted then unlocked the door, listened for a moment and stepped outside.

He closed the door with hardly a sound.

And he hoped upon hope that he had done the right thing.

．　　　．　　　．　　　．　　　．

There were two ways out from the foot of the stairs, and Rollison saw the porter near the front door, with a newspaper in front of his face—so close that it looked as if he was dozing. Rollison did not put that to the test, but turned in the other direction, a side door to the reception desk and keys. He had a spare car key, so crept out the back way, found the door which Lessing had left unlocked and stepped out. Soon he was in the yard, where the Rolls-Bentley was parked with a dozen other cars; and parked so that he could drive straight out. There was no sign of anyone about. He was able to open the parking-yard door from the inside, and five minutes after he had left Guy Lessing and his bride, was heading for the open road. His head was tender but not aching badly, and although his left wrist had little strength, the car's power steering made effort unnecessary. No police were watching the back of the hotel, and a policeman who was in the High Street, flashing a light on the door of a shop, took no notice of him beyond a casual stare.

"The one man who'll hate me for this is Lorne," Rollison said to himself; his smile was not wholly free from anxiety.

Was Lessing a sick man?

Could schizophrenia be ruled out?

Was Barbara safe with him?

Rollison felt as sure as a man could be that there was not the slightest danger for Barbara; as sure as he could be without absolute proof that Lessing had told the truth about tonight; and the arguments that the marriage with Helen Goodman had been impossible, seemed convincing.

So—who had married the woman?

Her killer?

Who would wed the girl under another man's name?

.   .   .   .   .

Rollison drove along the deserted roads, meeting hardly a car on the way. It was half-past two when he turned into Gresham Terrace, parked the car under a lamp where he need not leave the lights on, and went up to his flat. He let himself in. He felt very tired, now, and for the past hour had felt as if something was hitting him behind the eyes. He did not look into Jolly's room, but went straight to his own, and switched on the light. It hurt his eyes even more. He contemplated himself in the mirror; tail coat, fancy waist-coat, crumpled trousers, shoes dirty with the soil of the forest and the dust of the gravel. At least he hadn't to unfasten his tie. He began to ease his coat from his shoulders when he heard a sound at the door.

"Is that you, Jolly?"

"Yes, sir," said Jolly, coming in. He looked tired and pale in his blue dressing-gown and lighter blue pyjamas, but became wide awake when he surveyed the Toff. "Allow *me*, sir," he said, and began to help Rollison to undress. "Have you seen a doctor about that head wound?"

"Yes," answered Rollison, "and I ought to see one about my general state of mental health."

"A good night's rest will work miracles, sir."

"Not with an addle-pated jackass like me," said Rollison. "Where am I most likely to get inside information about Major Lessing?"

Jolly considered as he drew Rollison's arms out of his shirt sleeves; considered as he pulled off the striped trousers; considered while he fetched a pair of laundry-fresh pyjamas of apple green.

"Presumably from Major Lessing himself, sir."

"Or his flat. The one he shares with Major Carruthers."

"Quite," said Jolly. "In the morning——"

"Jolly," said Rollison urgently, "in the morning Major

Lessing may be under arrest. In the morning, his wife or his not-wife will be in the greatest possible distress. We must act promptly." He struck an attitude.

"But Mr. Rollison, you are in no condition——"

"If I'd had any sense at all I would have lifted his keys," complained Rollison. "Give me a coat shirt so that I don't have to draw it over my head."

"Sir, I beg you to rest."

"You seem to forget that people who have been injured in the head might become schizophrenic, and go round marrying all over the place," said Rollison. He was unnaturally alert, and now that his mind was needle sharp, too many thoughts crowded it. "How would you like it if I produced a couple of wives to take over the kitchen? That cellular shirt will do, and the thing I brought from America and you always call the blouse—thanks," added Rollison, allowing himself to be helped into the fresh clothes, and silent on his victory. "A pair of light shoes, tennis shoes, say. Do you want to be in on this excursion, or are you going back to bed?"

"I positively refuse to allow you to go meandering about Mayfair on your own in your condition." Jolly had never been more vehement.

"You make it sound as if I'm going to have twins," grinned Rollison. "I can't understand why I feel so bright, it must have been the milk down Hampshire way. Get the skeleton keys, Jolly. There's one thing, we're not likely to be accused of burgling the flat, even if we are caught."

"I am coming almost to believe anything," Jolly retorted, and there was bitterness in his voice, but he made no further protest. "Will you allow me time to dress, sir?"

"Put on a pair of old trousers and a polo sweater, and relax," urged Rollison. "By the way, did you ask Grice about Holy Joe?"

"Mr. Grice wasn't in, sir, and I thought it wiser not to ask a subordinate."

"You're probably right," Rollison agreed. "We'll try to find Holy Joe after this visit. Get busy, man!"

Ten minutes later, they went downstairs. No one was about, and London seemed to be a city of the dead. Jolly climbed into the Rolls-Bentley and took the wheel as Rollison went to the other side. Jolly drove off, expertly, first towards Piccadilly, then towards Park Lane and eventually towards that rabbit warren of streets and squares, of roads and mews, which make up the heart of Mayfair. The car purred through the silence, the pale street-lamps cast grey and rakish shadows, and ten minutes after they had left the house, Jolly stopped at the entrance to one of the smaller mews.

"Thanks," said Rollison. "Major Carruthers is out of the country, isn't he?"

"So I understand, sir."

"With luck I'll have found anything there is to find in half an hour," said Rollison. "Will you wait here?"

"If I come with you, we may be finished much more quickly," said Jolly. "I am really perturbed about your head wounds, sir."

"All right, park the old wreck and follow me," said Rollison. He climbed down carefully, still unable to take liberties, but feeling better than he had hoped and much better than Jolly feared. The cobbles of the mews were uneven and made walking difficult, but did not slow him down. He reached the four short steps leading to the flat where the number 3 showed clearly, for there was a lighted gas-lamp at the end of the mews. Rollison studied the lock, and was not surprised to find that it was old-fashioned, and should surrender easily to the skeleton key. He slid it in dexterously, heedless of making a sound, and before Jolly was half-way across the mews, had the lock back and the door open. He stepped into a small, dark hall. He did not know this flat well, but had been here several times, and remembered the lay-out : there were two bedrooms, a large drawing-room and a dining alcove and enough of everything else for hygiene and comfort. He stepped towards the draw-ing-room, where he knew he would find a writing-desk, and Jolly came in at the front door.

Then a light went on in one of the bedrooms, visible at the side and the foot of the door.

11

3, HEDDLE MEWS

"So Major Carruthers isn't away," Rollison said in a whisper. "You nip out, Jolly, I'll handle him." He had a finger on a light switch, but didn't press it down. Jolly skipped, remarkably nimble, to the front door, and pulled it to; but he did not close it. There was a scuffling sound inside the room where the light had gone on, and then the door was opened swiftly.

A *woman* stood there.

She was alone but not unprotected, for in her right hand was a small automatic. Her hand was steady. Rollison could not see her face properly, because the light was behind her, but what he could see was attractive. So, by the same guesswork, was her figure.

"Don't move !" she ordered.

"I swear I won't," said Rollison humbly.

The light shone on to his eyes and was painful; he felt them smarting and beginning to water. The woman raised the gun, and for a frightening moment he thought that she was going to use it.

She said, "Aren't you Rollison?"

That was cause for relief.

"Yes," he answered simply.

"What are you doing here?"

"I came to get something that Major Lessing left behind."

"Why couldn't he come himself?"

"It was a little difficult," answered Rollison, still not quite sure of this woman's mood : she looked as if she would be quite prepared to shoot if she thought it necessary. She was of medium height, wore a dressing-gown clutched tightly round the waist with her free hand, and it bulged so much at the front that he now had no doubt that she had quite a remarkable figure.

Maid?

Mistress?

"Why was it so difficult?"

"A man on his honeymoon——" began Rollison, and almost at once wished he hadn't, for that gun moved, and for a second time he was afraid that she was going to use it. She pointed it at his chest as she said :

"Don't try to be funny."

"It's the last thing I intended," Rollison answered her, and then decided that it was time he asserted himself. So he smiled and moved forward a little, winning the satisfaction of seeing her move away. Perhaps she wasn't as dangerous as he had thought. "Would you mind answering a question?"

"Try me."

"Why are you here?" asked Rollison simply. "In Major Lessing's flat?"

He prayed that she would explain by correcting him and naming Carruthers.

She stared at him.

"Why shouldn't I be?" she demanded. "I'm his wife, I'd like to know who has a better right."

.   .   .   .   .

Maid?

Mistress?

Wife?

Very little had made sense since Barbara had arrived in such a state of agitation at Rollison's flat, and this made less sense than anything that had gone before. Rollison gaped into the woman's face. She glowered at him, as if she saw nothing nonsensical in the situation. She had achieved a remarkable thing, for she had made him speechless; but obviously she did not intend that he should be speechless for long.

"What is all this nonsense about a honeymoon?" she demanded.

"Don't you ever read the newspapers?" Rollison asked, and tried not to sound banal.

"What difference does that make?"

"I hoped it would make a lot." The story of the wedding and pictures of both bride and groom were bound to be in the evening papers. "Isn't there one here?"

"No," she said, looking startled. "There is only a Paris morning newspaper. I flew over this afternoon. Do you mean——?"

"He means that you have been betrayed, woman!" a man boomed, and Rollison, taken completely off his guard, recognised the deep, damnation voice of Holy Joe. A door opened at Rollison's side, and the bearded man appeared, eyes glowing, lips parted, right hand raised as if for silence. "He means that you have been the victim of base, wicked man, that——"

"Joe! Be quiet!" the woman ordered.

"I will not be silenced by the whim of a woman," the bearded man declared, on a lower key. "Lessing has lived a double life. Keeping you in Paris, he has seduced a child——" He broke off.

"*This woman lives in Paris,*" Rollison thought, almost desperately, "*and Guy goes over to Paris every other week or so.*"

"Joe, what are you talking about?" demanded the woman who called herself Lessing's wife. "I don't believe——"

"Whether you believe it or not, it is the truth," growled Joe.

"Mr. Rollison, is he serious?" the woman demanded.

Rollison stood watching her, and watching Holy Joe. He felt the wind from the front door, which swung open a little wider; Jolly would be listening intently to all this, and would even risk being seen. Outside was London, sleeping;

all the ordinary people, normal, friendly, unaware of the fantastic situation in their midst.

"It's true," Rollison answered.

"And the wrath of the Lord is being felt upon us," declaimed Holy Joe, his eyes glistening. "Already death has been the reward of one sinful woman——"

"That's enough, Joe," Rollison said. "Who paid you to go shouting outside the church this morning? And what are you doing here?"

"This poor betrayed vessel has befriended me," boomed Holy Joe. "I came to break the news of her husband's crime gently, but you have compelled me to be harsh. Rose, be brave, my dear."

Rollison had a feeling that he was wholly phoney, and that now he was deliberately causing a distraction. Why? The woman still held the automatic, but it pointed towards the floor. She seemed bewildered, and that wasn't surprising. If she identified Guy Lessing as her husband, then the case was over.

Could she identify Guy? He thought that she looked scared; and who could blame her? She glanced towards the door, as if she thought that someone might come in to help her out of this bewilderment, and then looked back at Rollison, ignoring Holy Joe. She had clear brown eyes, not quite honey-coloured, and they showed very bright, as if because of her fear; and certainly because there was a slight trace of eye-shade on the lids and at the lashes.

"I don't believe it," she said at last, and then dropped on to the side of the bed; it was turned down and the sheet was rumpled, but it hardly looked slept in. Over a chair hung some stockings, on the chair were bra, panties, a girdle, a pot of cold cream. She put the gun down, as if it no longer mattered.

"Keep away from that gun, Joe," Rollison warned, and then raised his voice. "Jolly!" He wanted Jolly to take both gun and Joe, leaving him to talk with the woman.

Jolly didn't answer.

"Jolly!" called Rollison more sharply.

The only sound outside might have been a stifled cry.

"What's that?" the woman cried.

Then Holy Joe turned and raced out of the bedroom towards the front door, and he slammed the bedroom door in Rollison's face.

Rollison swung round, opened it and reached the passage. He saw the front door close; it slammed. He heard Holy Joe running across the cobbles as he ran to the front door, and snatched it open.

He fell headlong, for Jolly lay huddled at the top of the steps, while Holy Joe and another man ran away. Rollison could see them both, as they neared a corner.

12

GETAWAY

There was Jolly lying there, hurt, perhaps badly hurt; and there were the fleeing men. Holy Joe disappeared first; the other, near the corner of the mews, was running fast, his shadow foreshortened because he was almost beneath the lamp; a short, dark man who ran with hardly a sound.

A man had crept up upon him, Rollison, at Rufus Cottage, and struck him down before he had suspected danger.

Should he give chase?

He dropped on to one knee beside Jolly, and there was fear in him, for he saw the blood, dark and shiny, on the top step. He saw the gash in the side of Jolly's head, and then realised that the ear had been cut and most of the bleeding came from there. He felt for his man's pulse, and it was beating almost as steadily as it should be.

He stood up and ran down the steps.

He knew that he hadn't any hope of catching the assailant, for he simply could not run without his head lifting off his shoulders. He slowed down. It was infuriating, but there was nothing he could do about it, except try to reach the street to see if the men escaped in a car; if he could get the number of a car there might be a hope of tracing them.

He heard a car engine start off, reached the end of the mews and stepped into the street beyond, one which led to a graceful square now almost in darkness. A red light glowed, but the car was too far away for him to see the number, and it moved away.

He saw no sign of Holy Joe, who was almost certainly in the car. Undoubtedly, he had held Rollison's attention while Jolly had been attacked; and probably the other man had come to make sure that Holy Joe could get away.

That meant that the flat had been watched; and it made the prophet of woe a different, almost sinister figure.

Rollison turned back, walking very slowly.

Jolly still lay unconscious, and had not moved. As Rollison drew near, he realised with a shock that the woman hadn't come out to see what was the matter. Why not? Rollison quickened his pace, in spite of the lifting sensation in his head. He stepped over Jolly; he must soon pick him up, get him into the flat and dress that wound. There seemed to be no more bleeding.

He called, "Are you there?" because it was impossible to make himself say, "Mrs. Lessing."

There was no answer.

Did she think she could hide from him? Had she locked herself in her bedroom, and locked herself away from what she must know to be the truth?

The bedroom door was open; and so was the kitchen-door, as Holy Joe had left it. He could see a sink, a gas-stove, taps glistening like silver—and a wide-open window. He found himself almost gasping for breath as he passed the bedroom door; and then he stopped.

There she lay.

Dead?

He stood on the threshold of the room and stared at her. She lay on her side, and a silk stocking, *her* silk stocking, was twisted viciously round her neck and embedded in the white flesh. It could only have been done a matter of minutes, there must be time to save her. Someone had come in by the kitchen window and attacked her—and Holy Joe had probably known the man was coming.

Rollison lifted the woman bodily to the bed; she was very heavy. Her arms and legs flopped, and so did her head; and on the instant he knew that there was no chance for her, for her neck was broken.

He did not even know her real name.

Her voice seemed to echo in his ears.

"I'd like to know who has a better right. I'm his wife."

He felt her pulse, and it was not beating.

There was the desperate need to find Holy Joe; and the sickening realisation that for the second time inside twelve hours, he was by the side of a murdered woman— in circumstances which pointed suspicion at him.

He tried to remember what he had handled in this flat, and assured himself that there was very little. He left the motionless figure on the bed and looked about him, then espied the woman's handbag, on the dressing-table. He used a handkerchief as a glove, to open it without leaving prints, and found it crammed with oddments like lipstick and compact, purse and loose money; and there was a single letter. He had no time to spare, and snatched the letter out.

It was addressed to Major Carruthers, at 79 Rue de Gaspin, Paris, 6e.

He looked inside the envelope; there was a bill from a Paris garage. He put it back into the handbag, and hurried out to Jolly; Jolly was stirring now, making a little grunting noise. Rollison made a great effort, lifted him, hoisted him high and staggered with him down the steps. At a time when he wanted to be at his fittest, he was as weak as a child. He stumbled over the cobbles, but did not slip, and reached the car. He stood Jolly against it as he opened a rear door, and Jolly muttered :

"Quite all right, sir."

"Take it easy," Rollison said. "Try to raise your leg, and get in." He helped Jolly, whose limbs seemed like jelly, until he was squatting on the seat. "Just relax," Rollison added. He closed the rear door, and took the wheel. He looked up and down the street, fearful that a policeman might come and recognise the car, for it was well known in Mayfair. He saw no one, but could not be sure that no policeman had passed in the past twenty minutes. He started the self-starter, blessing the fact that it made hardly any noise.

He drove away, heading for Shepherd Market, where he knew he would find a telephone kiosk. He jumped out, stepped into a kiosk, dialled 999, and when a girl answered, he said in a hoarse voice :

"Send the police to 3, Heddle Mews, off Heddle Street. Murder."

"Wh——"

He rang off on the girl's word, and went back to the car. Jolly was sitting up and he could see the light glinting on his man's eyes; but Jolly made no attempt to speak until they reached Gresham Terrace. Rollison parked exactly where he had left the car before, and then helped Jolly out. Jolly asked no questions, but walked of his own accord towards the front door of Number 22. No one was in sight. Once they were indoors, they went upstairs one at a time; and Jolly was gasping for breath when they reached the top, while Rollison was almost normal.

Odd : his head felt easier.

He opened the door for Jolly, who went ahead and actually muttered, "I beg your pardon, sir." He was still unsteady.

"Bathroom," ordered Rollison.

The cut over Jolly's ear was nasty, and there was a swelling and a ragged-looking wound, but the blow had not gone very deep. Rollison bathed it, using an antiseptic, and then examined it critically.

"I shall put on some of the penicillin ointment which Dr. Marples prescribed for you, sir, and not dress it," Jolly announced, in a firm but subdued voice. "I am extremely sorry that I was unable to give you any warning. The man came upon me without making the slightest sound. Are *you* all right, sir?"

"I'm improving in everything but spirit," Rollison answered grimly. "How much did you hear at the flat?"

"Very little, sir, although enough to understand that the

woman actually claimed to be Major Lessing's wife. It really *is* ludicrous."

"Jolly," Rollison said, "Holy Joe was there too, and he told me she was Mrs. Lessing."

He told Jolly what else he knew, and added:

"It's a fact that while I was bending over you and chasing after your assailant, Wife Number Three was murdered. Not by Holy Joe, but presumably by an accomplice. I called the police, they'll have been with her for twenty minutes by now."

Jolly did not comment.

Rollison emptied the hand basin of the pink water, washed his own hands, then rinsed his face with cold water. He could move with greater freedom than before, as if the worst effect of his own wounds were past. He dried himself gently with a white towel, and when he put it aside, Jolly was sitting on the edge of the bath, staring at him.

"You see what I mean," Rollison said. "I was at the cottage when Wife Number 2 was killed—or about the same time, anyhow. And again with Number 3. Unfortunate, isn't it?"

"Do you think you left any evidence, sir?"

"I shouldn't think so," Rollison said, and made himself smile. "Pray for me. There is one thing."

"What is that, sir?"

"Major Lessing could not have killed this woman."

"Are you sure, sir?"

"I don't believe he would leave Mr. Lorne's daughter again tonight," Rollison said with great precision. "Jolly, what have we run into?"

"A very disturbing situation indeed," said Jolly, and stood up quite briskly. "I think we ought to put the lights out, sir. If the police associate this with the earlier murder, they will probably come round here, and if they see lights on they might put two and two together."

"Put 'em out," Rollison said. "And you aren't having a lucky night. I want you to go out, find a taxi, and visit

Croby's and Old Mike's doss-houses. If Holy Joe's at either, bring him back. If he objects, say you'll call the police. If you can't find him, telephone me to say so."

"Very good, sir," said Jolly. "It won't be easy to sleep, I'm afraid."

"Easy!" echoed Rollison, and gave a queer little laugh. "There's something we agree about. I wonder if the police will come round. If they do, it means they know I left Winchester, and that would suggest they'd been watching me all night. What do we hope, Jolly?"

"That they don't come here," Jolly said fervently.

. . . . . .

Half an hour later, he telephoned to say that Holy Joe was at neither of the doss-houses.

"Call the Yard, and tell Information that Holy Joe was in Heddle Mews tonight," Rollison said. "The police might be able to trace him."

. . . . . .

The police surgeon, who had arrived soon after the police at Heddle Mews, stood back from the body of the woman and said formally that she was dead. The three plain-clothes detectives who were in the room did not need telling that. They were already working, and others were on the way, from *Fingerprints* and *Photographs*. An ambulance was outside. One of the detectives was looking through a writing-desk in the big room, and he came hurrying into the bedroom, with a letter in his hand.

"Do you know who lives here?"

"A man named Carruthers, Major Carruthers."

"And a Major Lessing."

"*What?*"

"I thought that would shake you," the first man said. "We're looking for Lessing because of the New Forest job, and now we run into this. Now we really want the major, I hope they make this a hanging job." He went to the telephone, and then turned away. "Better not touch that, I'll use my radio phone outside. There's one thing, we needn't worry about Rollison, he's safely tucked up in Winchester."

One of the others said, "I wouldn't take that for granted."

"Had it from Reno, at Winchester, he actually put Rollison's car away," the man answered.

"That's funny." The one who did not believe that Rollison should be taken for granted frowned at the man who had discovered Lessing's name here. "I could have sworn I saw Rollison's Bentley on the road a couple of hours ago, I'd been out to Ealing. Think we ought to check?"

"Might as well," the other man said.

More police arrived, in two cars, and messages began to fly to and from Scotland Yard, the flat was buzzing with busy men, the body was taken away to the nearest morgue, and two policemen in a car drove round to Gresham Terrace. One of them knew Rollison's car, and as they drew alongside it, he said without hesitation :

"Reno may have put that car away in Winchester, but Rollison took it out again. Going to talk to him?"

"No," the first man said, very thoughtfully. "I don't think we will. We'll report back, and leave this to the Yard to handle. They're used to Rollison, and they've got the New Forest case on the go as it is. The less the Division has to do with this job, the less our headache will be." He switched on his radio, called the Yard and left the message.

. . . . . .

Rollison and Jolly, who was back at the flat, were quite unaware of all of this.

. . . . .

The first thing that Rollison did when he woke next morning a little after eight o'clock was to put a call in to the Roebuck Hotel. If he asked for the room number and if necessary for himself, he would be put through to Lessing, and the telephone operator would not think that anything was amiss. He had to be very guarded in what he said, and the essential thing was to assure himself that Lessing was still at the hotel. He felt bleary-eyed, and his head was much worse than it had been under the stimulus of last night's pressure. He put on a kettle, glad that Jolly was still asleep, and then made the telephone call.

He was soon through to the hotel.

"One moment, sir," a woman said brightly, and Rollison heard the sound as the plug was put in.

He waited impatiently.

He waited tensely.

He waited so long that he could hear the kettle hissing in the kitchen, and until he felt that he could fling the receiver down.

Then the woman operator said, "I'm sorry, sir, but Mr. Rollison doesn't seem to be in the hotel. There's no answer from his room, and he's not in the dining-room. If he comes in, can I get him to call you?"

"Nice of you," said Rollison. "But no, thanks. I'll call again after breakfast."

"If I can leave a message——"

"Ask him to call this number, will you?" asked Rollison, and gave the number of the flat, then rang off and hurried out to make the tea. He peered into Jolly's room; and Jolly looked as if he was likely to sleep for hours. Rollison drank two cups of hot tea, looking at the telephone most of the time, but it did not ring.

Why hadn't Lessing answered?

He would have answered had he been in the room, so the simple explanation was that he hadn't been there.

Had Barbara?

Had she refused to answer, fearful that a woman's voice would have aroused suspicion? Or had she been out too?

If so, when had they left?

Last night, or in the early hours? In time to be at Heddle Mews when the woman had been killed?

13

WAKING

BARBARA felt as if she could never open her eyes, she was
so tired, and the lids were so heavy, but it did not matter,
because there was no hurry. There would never be any
hurry. She was aware of light, not too bright, certainly not
waking her up. She heard a clatter of sound, as from a long
way off, without realising that it was in the yard of the
hotel; she did not at first realise that she was in the hotel,
just that she was so drowsy, heavy-eyed and determined to
drop off to sleep again.

Then, she thought, "Guy!"

She groped to one side, and her hand went over the edge
of the bed. She turned round in a flurry of eagerness mingled
with anxiety; her hand touched cold sheets, and she saw
only the rumpled pillow. The bedclothes had been drawn
up over her, she could tell that.

Bless him.

He would be in the bathroom.

She stared at the door, which was closed, and told herself that there was no need to call out, he would soon be
in. She *was* married. That running away was part of a
nightmare, like everything that had followed. She had no
sense of shock or dismay now, because she was quite sure
that whatever happened, Guy would come out of it well.
He would always come out of everything well.

Bless him.

Her eyes were still heavy, but her mind was alert and
active. She remembered everything that had been said before Rollison had left, and the fact that Rollison had gone
off and left them together was a clear indication of what he

thought: had he believed that Guy was already married, he would have slept in the armchair and probably made Guy sleep in the bathroom!

She smiled.

Guy hadn't!

If only ecstasy could last for ever . . .

Rollison was wonderful; she should have trusted him more, but if she had, if she hadn't taken it into her head to come down to the cottage, then last night would not have happened, and she would have spent her wedding night alone.

She hadn't.

Oh, Guy, love me always!

She was smiling to herself, and her eyes were wide open now, gently tired but no longer as heavy as lead. Her mouth was dry, and when she heard a maid walking along the passage, cups rattling on a tray, she wondered if she should press the bell and get some tea as a surprise for Guy.

She had better not; Rollison was supposed to be in this room, and Guy—well, Guy was wanted for questioning.

The first real shadow of the morning entered her mind. She had known that before, but had been able to thrust it aside, but now it harassed her. That Helen woman had been murdered, and Guy had been near the forest. It was hardly surprising that the police suspected him.

And suspected her, too.

The only wise thing was to leave everything to Rolly. She reminded herself again that he would not have left her and Guy alone unless he had felt absolutely sure that Guy was wholly innocent, and while he might have an occasional black-out, he could never have prepared that other marriage, laid all the plans, gone through with the ceremony and seen the woman from time to time—*always* in a black-out.

Guy had no split mind.

Barbara heard nothing from the bathroom, and realised that she had been lying here for five or six minutes, expecting the door to open, but seeing it closed all the time. She heard no splashing. Well, men didn't splash while they shaved, and Guy might be a very thorough shaver. He always looked as if he'd shaved a few minutes before he met her, he was one of those men who managed always to be immaculate.

But he wouldn't take so long shaving.

No water was running, there was no suggestion of splashing, no sound at all.

Barbara flung the bedclothes back.

That was when she realised that she had nothing on. She felt herself colouring furiously, tried to laugh the embarrassment away and stretched out for the tartan jacket. She slipped it on, and caught sight of herself in the mirror, long legs bare, jacket fitting rather like a three-quarter-length coat now that she hadn't pouched it, like a blouse. It would do, but what a honeymoon nightdress!

She could not make herself smile as she reached the bathroom door.

Should she tap?

She listened, but heard no hint of sound. Now she began to fear the worst, that Guy was not here. She opened the door an inch, and there was still no sound.

"Guy."

When there was no answer she pushed the door wide, and saw the thing she most feared: an empty bathroom.

Of course he hadn't shaved, he'd had no shaving gear, there was nothing here but the hotel towel and soap. The towels were all used, and they had left one untouched last night, so he had got up, washed, and—gone.

"But Guy," Barbara said, in a strangled voice.

Absurdly, she stepped right into the bathroom and looked behind the door. Then she went back into the bedroom, and she felt as if she were suffocating, this was so bitterly disappointing. She stood and looked round, while the noises came in at the open window—the window through which he had climbed. He had told her about that; she had woken up when he had started arguing with Rollison, not before; but afterwards, snuggling together, he had told her and they had hugged each other as they had laughed.

Then she saw the note, on the dressing-table; sight of it seemed to paralyse her. A note, on their first morning. Why couldn't she make herself go forward and pick it up, wrench it open, see what he had to say? What could he say, to explain such a thing as this?

She went forward, and her fingers were unsteady as she opened the envelope—an old envelope, addressed to him at his club, with that crossed out and her name written in pencil, just: *Barbara.*

She unfolded the letter inside.

It was on the back of one written to him, and all it said was in two sentences :

"I'll be back just as soon as I can clear myself. I can't involve you any more deeply.
All love,
Guy."

She read it and read it and read it again. The word all took on a great significance. "All" love; as she felt for him. But why hadn't he trusted her? Why hadn't he realised after last night that all she wanted to do was to share everything with him : anxieties, dangers, the good and the bad. Hadn't they sworn to do so yesterday, before the bishop, before the altar, in front of those hundreds of people, with her father standing by her side, a rather stern little ball of a father whom she loved so much.

Why hadn't Guy trusted her?

She turned the letter over, and on the other side was a note scrawled in a handwriting she didn't recognise, but she knew it was from Ralph Carruthers; that was the only Ralph she had heard Guy mention, and the letter was signed just with that Christian name.

"I'll be away most of the next three months, the cottage and the flat are yours, old boy. If I'm coming home unexpectedly I'll give you some warning. Yours aye, Ralph."

Ralph Carruthers, Barbara repeated to herself drably, as if the name really meant something. The letter was dated three weeks earlier, so Guy had carried it about with him all that time. Probably he had kept it in his wallet, and transferred it from suit to suit.

Where was he?

She went to the window, but no ladder was there; it looked as if Guy had climbed down it, then put it in its usual place.

She looked at her watch, the only thing she had worn which she hadn't bundled up and left at Winchester Station. It was five to eight. She was surprised that she had woken so early, although at least she understood why she had felt so heavy-eyed. Now she felt as if she would never be able to close her eyes again. She went into the bathroom, hesitated and decided not to bath. She washed hurriedly, dressed in a few minutes and looked at herself in the mirror of the large oak wardrobe.

"No wonder he ran away," she said. "I look like a schoolgirl in pants."

She had not put on her bra, so as to look like a boy more convincingly. Well, she could, and proved it when she put the cap on, pulling it well down over her ears so that no one could see that her hair was not cut short.

She drank two glasses of cold water.

The obvious thing to do was to get in touch with Rollison, but a deep fear was driving her all the time: that the police would suspect that she was involved, and that once she was recognised, they would arrest her; or at least take her to the police-station for questioning. There were a lot of questions she did not want to answer. She wished that she could go and hide herself for days, for weeks, for months if necessary, until it was all over, and she could begin life with Guy.

She stepped to the door.

It wasn't locked; of course, Guy could not have locked it from the outside, even if he'd gone out by the door; he had been forced to let her get out without calling for someone to let her out, for the hotel people thought Rollison was in this room.

Now all that Barbara could think of was Rollison.

She heard nothing, opened the door, stepped swiftly into the passage and closed the door again. As it closed, a maid turned the corner, making hardly a sound, carrying only some towels.

"Good morning, sir."

Barbara grunted, deep as she could, " 'Morning."

The maid seemed to notice nothing amiss. Barbara went towards the stairs, feeling as if every door was hiding a policeman who would open it and pounce on her. She reached a landing, and a man and woman, young, clear-eyed, obviously happy, were coming along another passage, hand-in-hand; as she should be with Guy. She let them go down first; at least they were not interested in her. But two big men stood in the hall, one talking to a receptionist, another reading a newspaper. Undoubtedly they looked like detectives. She held her breath as she reached the foot of the stairs. If either of them spoke to her, she would panic and give herself away; she just wouldn't have a chance.

The first man stared at her over the top of his newspaper. The other glanced round, as if uninterested.

She made herself walk slowly. The swing doors seemed a mile away, and the bright sunlight outside seemed to mock her. Every step took an age and her feet were like lead, but she did not stop, and reached the door without being called.

She pushed the door, and one of the sections banged against her heel as she squeezed through. Once on the pavement, she felt as if she must turn and run, she was so sure that one of the men would follow her; but neither did.

She knew where the station was, from here, and turned towards it. Half-way along the street, she saw a policeman walking across the road towards her. She had the feeling that she must run again, but conquered panic, and the policeman passed, looking at her keenly; and looking at her more as a man might look at a pretty girl.

Well, he hadn't stopped her.

She quickened her pace, no longer feeling that she was being watched. She was able to breathe more easily. She had plenty of money, thirty pounds or more in her purse, which was in a pocket of the tartan coat. It was very hot, and she wished she could take the coat off, but she dared not chance that.

She reached the station, and bought a second-class ticket to Waterloo; there was a train just after nine o'clock. She should be in London by half-past ten and would go straight to Rollison's flat.

What else could she do?

She bought a newspaper at a station bookstall. The news of the cottage murder was on the front page, but there was no mention of Guy and none of her. A Miss Helen Goodman had been murdered, according to the report, so the police had not released the news that Helen Goodman could also call herself Mrs. Lessing—or Smith.

Barbara looked at the stop press, and that was when her heart seemed to stop, for it read : "Police anxious to interview Major Guy Lessing and Mrs. Lessing formerly Barbara Lorne in connection with New Forest cottage murder."

Now the whole world knew.

She walked to the end of the platform, without looking round. She must get to London and see Rollison, he was the only man who could advise her what best to do.

She took no notice of the man who entered the station a few minutes after her. He glanced towards her, then bought a newspaper and strolled half-way between the bookstall and the end of the platform. He did not seem to be watching her, but suddenly she realised who it was.

This was the man who had looked at her over the newspaper at the hotel.

. . . . .

It was, in fact, Detective Inspector Reno of the Winchester C.I.D. An hour earlier, when the Winchester police had guessed what had happened after consultation with the Yard, Reno had said:

"The girl's masquerading as a boy, it's definitely her. I suspected it last night. She'll lead us to Lessing all right, we'd be wiser to follow her, not question her right away."

Now he read his second newspaper of the morning, but did not miss a single move his quarry made.

Half an hour later, he was sitting in the dining-car, watching her. She had her back towards him, and seemed to be making a good breakfast. Reno wondered if that meant anything; if she were really worried, wouldn't she have been put off her food?

Poor kid, thought Reno.

14

FRIGHTENED PARENT

"WHAT we have to find out for certain is whether the police know that we were at Heddle Mews last night," Rollison said, as he sat at his desk a little after ten o'clock that morning, with Jolly sitting on an upright chair, looking pale, and with a plaster over his right ear, which was padded to look like any prize-fighter's. "The odds are that they know what time we got home, the car would be recognised."

"The most they can do is guess, sir."

"They might decide that it's safe to act on guesswork," Rollison argued. His back was to the trophy wall, and the hempen hangman's rope seemed very close to the nape of his neck. He could not turn his right wrist with any comfort, but his left hand was much better, and he could clasp and unclasp the fingers. He looked little the worse for the battering, and had recovered much more quickly than Jolly, who looked positively old. "Jolly," went on Rollison, "wouldn't you think that Mr. Lorne would read the newspapers?"

"I've been wondering why he hasn't called," said Jolly.

All the six newspapers on Rollison's desk were late morning editions, and each carried the story of the mews murder as well as the murder in the New Forest. There was no mention or hint of Holy Joe. The fact that Helen Goodman had been secretly married to a Major Lessing had driven nearly every other story off the front pages. One headline read:

MAJOR WITH THREE WIVES

This was followed by a sub-heading almost as large:

TWO MURDERED

The other headlines were as bad. There were photographs, of Helen Goodman, the woman at the mews whose name was given as Rose Lessing, and Barbara; and Barbara was younger and more beautiful than the others. There was Lessing's photograph, and almost alongside it a story under the heading:

MODERN BLUEBEARDS . . .

In fact, everything was on the front pages, so the attempt at blackmail was stillborn; there had been no point in advising Lorne to send those hundred pounds out to the ten addresses.

Rollison got up and went to the window, standing to one side so that he could see into the street without being seen from it. No one appeared to be watching Number 22, but the police might have decided to play very cautiously. The Rolls-Bentley was still there. He came back from the window, and stood by the telephone; then he dialled Robert Lorne's number.

A man-servant answered.

"I'm sorry, sir," he said. "Mr. Lorne left the house early this morning, and did not say where he was going."

"How early is early?"

"A little after seven o'clock, sir. May I give him a message when he returns?"

"Tell him that Richard Rollison called. Have you heard anything from Miss Barbara this morning?"

"From Mrs. Lessing, sir? No, naturally not." There was reproof in that, and the man-servant said much more than the words. "There is nothing at all wrong," he seemed to say, "and everything will be fully explained when everything is known." Exactly what Jolly would have implied in similar circumstances. Rollison put the receiver down:

"First and last we want Guy Lessing," he said, and seemed to be talking to himself, "and——"

Jolly stood up.

"If you will forgive me, sir, I take a different point of view."

"What one?"

"We need Mrs. Lessing or Miss Lorne first."

Rollison said, "I suppose I've been boggling at this since I woke up, but give it me in words of three letters."

"A man who has killed two women might kill a third, sir."

"Not at all bad," said Rollison heavily. "No one could ask for simpler English. That puts the new bride in jeopardy."

"Don't you agree, sir?"

"I've known Major Lessing for thirty-three years."

"He *was* badly wounded."

"Yes. Did you know that he was almost entirely alone in the world, Jolly? That he lost his parents twenty-five years ago, that his only sister died twenty years ago and there are only distant relations."

"Yes, sir."

"So he hasn't many friends."

"If I may say so, sir, he was not very good at making friends."

"No. But he needs some. We are his friends."

"Very good, sir."

"The first thing we do is start the wires of Fleet Street working," Rollison said. "Call all of our contacts, and just state clearly the fact of this old wound, and add that Dr. Willard knows all about it. Get that done quickly. The evening newspapers should carry it, and tomorrow morning's will probably be running articles on the tragedy of wounds which catch up with their victim many years after they were inflicted. You could even suggest some articles like that."

"Very good, sir."

"Then we need to find his only other friend," Rollison went on, "Major Ralph Carruthers, who is probably in Paris. Isn't it a little odd, Jolly, that Mrs. Lessing the Second lived most of her time in Paris?"

"A coincidence, sir."

"An understatement. And Holy Joe knew that and knew the woman. I wish I knew where to lay my hands on him." He paused, and went on very thoughtfully, "I think that Major Carruthers is more likely to know where we might find Major Lessing than anyone else. Do we know Major Carruthers' Paris address?"

"I think we have a note of it, when he invited you to visit him if you were over there with any time to spare."

"I'll check," said Rollison. "You can get a seat on a Paris plane about the middle of the afternoon, the first available after four o'clock, say. Book it under the name of Smith."

"If the authorities are aware that you were in Heddle Mews last night, sir, they may not allow you to leave the country."

"Let's cross that stream when we get to it," said Rollison. He still seemed to be talking more to himself than to Jolly. "I wonder if they followed up the Holy Joe tip. One thing's certain, anyhow, they'll be watching Lorne's house, his club and his office. They'll be watching Major Lessing's club, too, and all the places he was known to frequent, and they'll cover every place where Lorne's daughter is likely to be. It would only be a waste of time if we also covered any of those places, so Major Carruthers seems to be our only angle, except Holy Joe, and I think we'll leave him to the police." Rollison took the first marriage certificate out of his pocket and studied it. "There is a chance that the Registrar will remember the marriage, but the police are probably on to that, too. Jolly."

"Sir?"

"Major Carruthers seems positively our only hope."

"Yes, sir."

"Make sure of the seat on that plane," urged Rollison, and then looked up sharply, for he heard footsteps outside. "I'll go, Jolly."

Jolly got up and approached the desk as Rollison went across the room, into the lounge hall and to the front door. The police might be there; Lorne; or Barbara. He looked into the mirror and saw Lorne.

When Rollison opened the door, Barbara's father gave the impression that he had not slept at all. His face was a little blotchy, but his hair was smoothed down and he was as immaculate as ever in a fine-textured pale grey suit, which made him look impossibly well dressed.

"Good morning," he said curtly, as he stepped in.

"Hallo," said Rollison, "I've been trying to get in touch with you."

"So I would expect." They went into the big room, and Lorne looked as if longingly at the trophy wall, and all the lethal weapons there. "I ought to have broken the swine's neck," he growled. "I take it that you have caught up with the night's news?"

"Yes."

"To think that my Barbara should get involved with a scoundrel who makes a habit of marriage." Lorne looked almost despairing. "Rollison, do you know where Barbara is?"

"No."

"You are hardly proving a brilliant detective."

"Bob," said Rollison mildly, "I expect you to be in a pretty miserable mood, but don't be awkward for its own sake. You could still be wrong about Lessing."

"Are you going off your head?"

"Not yet," said Rollison. "There's one possibility which you'd see yourself if you would only keep your eyes open, and try to see."

"I didn't come here to be insulted."

"Either you're not the man I think you are, or you didn't sleep last night," said Rollison placatingly. He wondered what Lorne would say if he knew that Barbara and Lessing had been together last night; and especially if he knew that he, Rollison, had made the reunion possible. The bright eyes with a glitter in them suggested that Lorne had been driven to distraction; goaded by such news as that, he would want to strike out and hurt.

Lorne said, "Oh, I'm sorry, but I hate the world this morning. What is this possibility that you're talking about?"

"That not Guy Lessing but someone masquerading as Guy Lessing married these other women."

Lorne opened his mouth, drew in a hissing breath and then said almost hysterically :

"Now I know you're a lunatic. Who in this wide world would do that? Who would even want to? What advantage would it be? For God's sake get this loyalty to Lessing out of your system. He's a rogue, he's a man who uses all his so-called aristocratic background to prey upon women, and if he were to walk into this room this moment I would thrash him with my own hands."

"You're behaving like a father out of a Victorian melodrama," Rollison protested, still mildly. "I know Guy Lessing, I can believe that he would think it quite normal and even proper to have a mistress tucked away in several different places, but——"

"Oh, stop bleating !" Lorne said roughly. "I've been checking, and I've found out about this head wound. I've no doubt that there will now be an attempt to whitewash him, saying that he's a hero suffering from the results of fighting for his country. But I know better. He's as sane as you or I—*if* you're sane—and he'll use this old wound to pretend that he didn't know what he was doing. I've just come from the surgeon who performed the operation on him, so I know the kind of argument that's likely to be used. I also know that he had been approached by Lessing's doctor, Willard, who is also a friend of yours. Deny that?"

"There's no reason why I should deny it," Rollison said.

He was beginning to find it difficult to keep his temper. Lorne seemed to have come determined to be cantankerous, and he should have more self-control. Certainly if he knew about last night——

There was a sharp ring at the front-door bell, and a moment later Rollison heard Jolly open the door, and then heard Barbara say:

"Is Mr. Rollison in, Jolly? I must see him."

"Barbara!" Lorne cried, and bounded towards the entrance hall before Rollison could move. Rollison reached the open doorway in time to hear Barbara exclaim, "Oh, Daddy!" and then to see them in each other's arms. Lorne was holding his daughter so tightly that it looked as if he meant to make sure she could never get away again.

But Barbara wasn't so happy about this reunion.

She looked over her father's head and into Rollison's eyes, and there was no doubt at all that she had read about the murder in the mews, and of the second Mrs. Lessing. She would hate telling her father the whole truth, and must be longing to get away.

Lorne released her.

"Now that you're back, you've nothing more to worry about," he said gruffly, and there were tears in his eyes. "Thank God you're all right. The man must be mad, but don't worry, Barbara my darling. We'll get out of the country for a month or two until it's all blown over, and there'll be no trouble in getting an annulment." He turned to Rollison, his face now wreathed in smiles that made him look younger and almost boyish. "Why didn't you tell me you were expecting Barbara?"

"Father," Barbara said; not Dad or Daddy now.

"You needn't worry at all," Lorne assured her. "There's nothing at all to worry about. I'll make quite sure that he can't do you any more harm. But thank God you were so lucky; that he didn't try to kill you."

"Father——"

Lorne seemed oblivious of the tension in her voice.

"The moment Lessing is under lock and key it'll all be over, and you'll have nothing at all to worry about I tell you. I'm sure that in spite of your understandable loyalty, you agree about that, Rolly." He was almost skittish.

"Father," Barbara said, very deliberately, "I don't like to hear you talking about my husband like that."

15

QUARREL

THERE was something almost comic about the change in Lorne's expression; and something pathetic, too. The girl sensed that. Jolly, who was discreetly out of sight, undoubtedly noticed it. Rollison watched father and daughter, so utterly unalike, and wondered whether Lorne would explode again; or whether he would be able to control himself more successfully with the girl.

He tried.

"Barbara, you don't know what you're saying."

"I know exactly what I'm saying. Guy is my husband."

"Barbara, don't be ridiculous. That isn't true."

"I don't believe that he ever knew those other women."

"Now don't be absurd," Lorne said sharply. "There are the certificates, the evidence of bigamous marriage, the evidence that he preyed on foolish women."

Barbara was going very white.

"Please don't go on, Father."

"I must, for your own good," Lorne said, only a little more gently. "I can understand him fooling you in the first place, although I never liked him, I never trusted him. Now we have all the evidence to prove how right I was. Why, the man is a cold-blooded murderer, killing two women to try to hide his crimes. How can you defend him?"

"I don't believe it's true."

"Now look here, my girl——"

"Don't stand there maligning my husband and 'my-girl-ing' me," Barbara said, and obviously she had great difficulty in keeping her voice steady. "You never liked him, you nearly put me against him."

"If you'd had any sense at all you would have listened."

"Don't keep calling me a fool!"

"I've called a spade a spade all my life, and I'm not going to stop now," Lorne said roughly. "I ought to have knocked the nonsense out of you. Why you hadn't the common intelligence to see through him I'll never know, you certainly didn't take after me. I ought to have known better than to let you mix with that set of decadent fools. Just because he can trace his ancestry back a few hundred years, and was educated——"

"Dad," Barbara said, and there was desperate appeal in her eyes as well as her voice, "don't keep on, I can't stand it."

"You've got to be made to understand that he's nothing but a swine."

"Don't talk like that about my husband," Barbara cried, and now her eyes were glittering.

Lorne's were as bright with battle.

"He's your husband only in name, and thank God the police will catch him before there's any chance of you——"

"We spent last night together!" cried Barbara. "Do you understand that spade? Now will you stop talking as if Guy's a criminal. I love him, I married him, I'd give my life for him. I don't believe all these lies!"

Lorne caught his breath, as if he were physically hurt. They stood glaring at each other, and to Rollison the real tragedy of this situation lay not in the death of two women, but in the breakdown between the relationship of father and daughter.

Lorne said, as if with an effort, "Where is he now?"

"I wouldn't tell you even if——"

"You wouldn't tell me even if you knew, is that it?" The man seemed to have shrunk physically. "So he has run away from you. He is a fugitive from justice. He is running away from the consequences of two murders. And you can stand there and defend him."

"He isn't a murderer."

"When you are in your right mind you can come and see me," Lorne said flatly. "Whatever folly you have committed, you are my daughter, and I shall give you all the help I can. Meanwhile, I shall do everything I can to help the police to find this wicked man." His voice was edgy, and his lips were trembling as he finished speaking and turned towards the door.

Jolly appeared in the hall, to open the front door for him. Barbara watched him, hard-eyed because she was so angry, and because her love was so deep. There were other things, obvious to the Toff. She had staked her faith and her future on this love, she had to be loyal to the man whom she had married; but there must be awful doubts in her mind, doubts forced even deeper by her father.

Jolly opened the door.

Lorne did not look round, and Barbara did not speak. Lorne went downstairs, and the closing of the door cut off his footsteps. There were tears in the girl's eyes when she turned towards the Toff, and she went to a chair and sat on the arm, pathetic, boyish except that she had pulled off the hat, and her lovely hair cascaded about her head and shoulders. Rollison thought that she was going to cry, but she did not; instead she actually managed a smile, and said :

"Does everyone agree with him?"

"Nearly everyone."

"Don't you?"

"I daren't."

She closed her eyes; that old and familiar trick.

"I know," she whispered. "I daren't, either." Now she looked at him. "Is there anything at all that I can do or you can do?"

"Do you know where Guy is?"

"No," Barbara answered, and when she saw doubt grow into his expression she spoke more firmly. "That's the truth, I wouldn't lie to you about it. He left before I woke up, and left a note on the dressing-table. Time-honoured, isn't it?" That was almost bitter. She waited while he read the note she handed to him, and then went on, "Can you think where he would go?"

"No," lied Rollison, and saw the way she stared, as if she realised that it wasn't the truth. There was a change in her expression now, a kind of thoughtfulness which hadn't been there before; obviously she had had an idea, but she didn't put it into words. "The important thing is to find him, Barbara. Where will you stay while you're in London?"

"I don't know. I'll find a hotel somewhere."

"I've an aunt who runs a kind of club," Rollison said. "It's called the Marigold Club. She'll have a spare room. You'll find it much better than a hotel, you'll get more privacy, and we can keep in touch easier. Will you go there?"

"I suppose I'd better," Barbara agreed, and then leaned forward. "I'm sorry, that wasn't very gracious. Yes, thank you, Rolly."

Undoubtedly her mood had changed, and Rollison was almost certain that it was because of that idea. He felt sure, too, that she believed that she knew where she could find Guy. Nothing would make her tell him, yet, in case he told the police. Now she had certainly ranged herself on Lessing's side, and nothing would shake her loyalty, because she dared not let it.

"I'll have a word with my aunt Gloria," Rollison said. "You'll probably find some clothes that will fit you in the spare room here"—he grinned—"and then Jolly can drive you round to the Club."

"I'd rather walk," Barbara said.

She did not want any escort, because she did not intend to go straight to the Marigold Club, Rollison knew. He said nothing to show what he suspected, but when she had gone into the spare room, hurrying, he called the Mayfair number of Lady Gloria Hirst, his favourite aunt.

She was in; she was helpful; of course she had read the

newspapers and knew that Richard was the centre of a
great deal of unwanted publicity again, no doubt the day
would come when he would grow out of these childish
escapades. Meanwhile, if the young woman had quarrelled
with her father and been deserted by her husband, then she
would be welcome.

"Glory, you're more wonderful than ever," Rollison said.
"She may know where Major Lessing is. If you could find
out——"

"I do *not* intend to act as a spy for you in one of your
ridiculous games," declared Lady Gloria tartly.

Rollison grinned, rang off and then went into the kitchen;
there Jolly, working at half speed, was trying to behave as
if this was a normal day.

"I should get something cold for lunch, and give priority
to that aircraft ticket," Rollison said. "As soon as Miss or
Mrs. L—good lord!"

Jolly watched him, as if expecting that exclamation to
herald an announcement of great significance; in fact, Jolly
looked almost eager.

"I've just thought of something," Rollison said. "Change
the name and not the letter, change for worse and not for
better. Jolly."

"Sir?"

"I am feeling quite well, thank you. I'd better go out
ahead of our guest, if I follow her from the door she'll
know what I'm going to do, and she's not a fool. Simple,
yes, but she has cunning. Tell her I've been called to Scotland Yard."

"Are you sure you feel well enough to go out, sir?"

"Yes," Rollison said, and his eyes kindled. "You take it
easy, Jolly, and if you get any pain from that wound, send
for Dr. Willard."

"I shall be perfectly all right, sir."

Rollison said soberly, "We're not so young as we used
to be. Don't overdo it."

"I'll contact Fleet Street as you advised, sir," Jolly

promised, as if he intended to demonstrate that he was still perfectly capable of carrying out his normal duties.

Rollison went out, and down the stairs.

He judged that Barbara would be another five minutes or so, time for him to get a taxi and to be at the end of the terrace ready to follow her; the taxi-drivers who used the nearby cab ranks were accustomed to his habits and his odd requests; and at this time of the morning he would have no difficulty in securing one. Provided he didn't try to turn his head, he felt quite fit. He reached the street, stepped into the bright sunlight and wondered if he was right about Barbara suddenly realising where she might find Guy. She had suddenly remembered the address of the cottage, and this suggested that she was subject to quick flashes of memory.

He saw a man sitting at the wheel of a large black car a few cars along; a man who was double parked. As he neared this car the man opened the door and got out.

"Hallo, Mr. Rollison."

"Ah," said Rollison solemnly. "Hallo, Reno, have you been transferred to the Yard?"

"We're working together on this job," answered Reno comfortingly. "How's Miss Lorne—or should I say Mrs. Lessing?"

"You should," said Rollison. "She's fine."

"I didn't think her father looked very happy when he left just now," said Reno. "One of my colleagues from the Yard told me who it was." Another man came strolling across the street, and now Rollison saw a third, at the corner —on the very route to the taxis he had come to get. "What time did you leave the Roebuck, Mr. Rollison? Before or after the unfortunate happening in Heddle Mews?"

"Before," said Rollison cautiously.

"We knew that, but I didn't expect you'd admit it so promptly," said Reno, whose manner was almost unbearably friendly. "Did you recognise the woman who called herself Mrs. Lessing—the *third* Mrs. Lessing?"

"Reno," said Rollison, with quiet urgency, "I want to follow the real, one and only Mrs. Lessing, she'll be leaving in a few minutes. She may know where her husband is."

"Odd thing, sir, but we had the same idea," Reno assured him, giving a grin which had become positively hateful. "In fact, I followed the young lady from Winchester this morning with the same possibility in mind. I believe my colleague has a warrant to search your flat, in case Mr. Lessing is hiding there—without your knowledge, of course! —and we'll look after the young lady. I know you'd do a much better job, but you can't be in two places at the same time, can you?"

Rollison said owlishly, "Two, Inspector?"

"Yes, sir." That was a detective sergeant from Scotland Yard. "I'd like you to come along to the Yard to answer a few questions, if that's all right with you."

"No doubt you'll have all the answers," Reno enthused.

It would be folly to try to avoid going to the Yard; folly to have the police on his heels. He would not be able to help the girl or Lessing; and would have no chance of flying to Paris and seeing Carruthers. There was a possibility that the police had already suspected that Carruthers might be able to help in this affair, but above everything else—even above seeing Holy Joe—Rollison wanted to go to Paris and find out for himself.

He still had time.

He smiled. "Of course," he said, "but if you let that girl get away, you might have a lot to answer for."

Reno's expression hardened; so did that of the Yard detective. It was Reno who said in a rough voice :

"We know we're up against a psychopathic case, and that Lessing goes around marrying women and then murdering them, and we aren't going to take a chance with this girl."

"If 'this girl' discovers she's being followed, she'll give you the slip," Rollison urged. "Don't take it too easily. And I won't hold that piece of indiscretion against you,

Reno, but a man is still innocent before he's proved guilty. If you really want to take me to the Yard, let's go."

"Right away," the Yard man said.

Then Rollison heard his name called, in Jolly's unmistakable voice, and he turned and looked up. His neck seemed to scream at him. He saw Jolly at the open window, waving; and then Jolly disappeared. He would be downstairs in a minute or less, and the police were too intrigued to make Rollison leave at once. He went with Reno and the detective sergeant to the front door, which opened swiftly, as Jolly appeared; and Jolly had forgotten his troubles in his haste.

"She's gone, sir," he burst out.

Rollison echoed, "Gone?"

"*Gone?*" gasped Reno.

"I was a little puzzled by the silence from the spare room, sir, and ventured to knock. There was no answer, so I looked in, and the room was empty. She had changed her clothes, the ones she was wearing were on the bed. I can only imagine that she went out by the fire-escape while I was on the telephone."

Rollison flashed, "Come on!"

He turned and ran; and the detectives followed him, while the man at the corner, who had been watching the turning from which anyone who left by the fire-escapes in Gresham Terrace would come, seemed in anguish.

He had not seen Barbara.

And she was nowhere to be seen.

. . . . .

"If she knows where Lessing is and has gone to him, God help her," Reno said.

16

POLICE QUESTIONS

SCOTLAND YARD was at once a familiar place and a strange one. There had been many changes of staff. The younger men knew of Rollison more by reputation than by experience. The senior officers, who had virtually grown up with the Toff, had mostly retired. His old and close friend, Superintendent Grice, was on holiday. Faces which he knew but which had neither sympathy nor understanding surrounded Rollison when he reached the Yard. He was seething with anger, and yet knew that Barbara might have slipped through any guard in like circumstances. She had gone into the flat wearing the tartan jacket and flannel trousers, left it wearing a decorous grey suit, as far as Jolly was able to say. She had probably worn a hat, too. And the detective on duty at the corner might have seen her without suspecting who it was; the distraction along Gresham Terrace had made the chance of that even greater.

Now, a Superintendent named Ellerby was saying:

"We know that there have been times when you've been able to achieve some results, Mr. Rollison, and we know you mean well. We also know you were at Heddle Mews last night—you left a print. Let's face it, we don't think you had anything to do with the murders, even though you were handy at the time of each. In fact, we think you probably suspected that murder would be attempted, and went to try to prevent it. That's why we're sore. If you did that, why didn't you tell us in advance? Haven't you yet come to realise that you can't play about with matters like murder?"

It would be easy to tell him that on the trophy wall there

were more souvenirs of murder cases than he, Ellerby, had handled in his fifteen years in the Criminal Investigation Department. It would be easy to rile Ellerby; and easier still to lose his own temper, so that he would become at logger-heads with the police. That would not help; only sweet reason would.

"Let's start with a clean sheet," Rollison said mildly. "I'd no idea that murder was contemplated. Barbara Lorne came to me and told me that she'd been told about this marriage to a woman from Bane. I knew from Lessing that he planned to go to the Bane cottage for his honey-moon, and . . ." Rollison was crisp and brisk, held Ellerby's attention, and just gave a shorthand-note taker time to get everything down. "After that, it was a question of believing that Lessing was a schizophrenic or a rogue, or else there was someone else behind all this whom no one knew. I went to Heddle Mews hoping to find people whom Lessing knew, and I didn't. I talked to the woman, who said she was his wife. Holy Joe appeared, and boomed a lot of nonsense." Rollison explained in some detail, and added grimly, "I wasn't at my liveliest, or I would have stopped Joe. Have you got him?"

"We acted on your tip, but we can't find him," Ellerby said. "There's a call out."

"That man's no slouch," Rollison observed heavily. "Do you know much about him?"

"Next to nothing," Ellerby answered frankly. "He's been in London on and off for years, but does most of his tramp-ing in the provinces, as far as we know—he's only here for the odd week or so now and again."

"Anything known against him?"

"He just goes around with his hell-and-damnation Crusade, that's all, we've always thought him a harmless religious fanatic. We've sent out the call to all the pro-vincial forces, too, so we ought to get some news soon. Now, you were telling me——"

"Yes," Rollison said, and went on: "My man was attacked outside . . ."

Soon Ellerby was asking pertinent questions: had Jolly seen his assailant, had there been one man or two besides Holy Joe, what had the woman said? Rollison answered frankly, and the atmosphere noticeably thawed.

"Of course you've had a lot of experience," Ellerby conceded, as man to man. He stood up from his big desk. "But you're strongly prejudiced in Major Lessing's favour."

"Yes."

"So it's no use asking your dispassionate opinion."

"I think Major Lessing is being impersonated."

Lorne had almost screamed ridicule, but Ellerby didn't. The Superintendent might be a big, tough-looking man, but his unexpectedly quiet voice and willingness to see reason made him much more likeable now than when Rollison had first arrived. He flipped over some memoranda on his desk, and remarked musingly:

"Either it's that, or he's mad. Have you seen the medical reports?"

"They might get him off on the grounds of insanity, but they'd only stand up if it was proved conclusively that he killed both women," Rollison said. "The timing at the mews is pretty close. I doubt if I was in London an hour before I started off for Carruthers' place—it may have been an hour and a half. I didn't drive fast, of course. He could have left an hour after me and reached London in time to kill the woman, but he had an alibi for the early part of last night."

"Seriously think the young woman's evidence would serve as an alibi?" asked Ellerby. "She's in love with him, and would obviously lie for him. Worried about her, Mr. Rollison?"

Rollison saw the trap, and walked into it.

"Very."

Ellerby said triumphantly:

"So you think Lessing may be ready to kill again?"

"I think the killer might be," Rollison retorted. "I still don't think Lessing's the killer."

"On what grounds?"

"Thirty-five years of acquaintance."

"No evidence?"

"Only your evidence."

"If I had to take this case to court tomorrow, I think I could make it stick," Ellerby declared, and Rollison believed that he meant it. "What do you want to do, Mr. Rollison?"

Rollison said slowly, "I think I want to be given a completely free hand to go where I like, in this country or out of it, with my assurance that if I find Lessing I'll report at once to you."

"Then why not tell us where you'd go to look for him, and let us go?"

"I think I could get a lot more out of him than you could, and that if I tell you in advance, you'll steal a march on me, and the damage will be done."

"You haven't much confidence in us, have you?" Ellerby was tart.

"I disagree with your theory on this case. You'll approach it from an angle I think is the wrong one, and could be dangerous."

"Will you leave the country, Mr. Rollison?"

"I might."

"Paris?"

So the police were on to that angle.

"Possibly."

"Mr. Rollison," said Ellerby, with a smile which was quite pleasant, "twenty minutes or so ago your man Jolly booked a seat on an aircraft leaving for Paris from London Airport at four o'clock this afternoon, an *Air France* Constellation. He booked it in the name of Smith. The booking clerk recognised his voice, knew that he usually made reservations for you and asked for a number to check back on.

Jolly gave your number. Are you going to see Major Carruthers?"

So Ellerby was good; if he claimed that he was quite competent to handle this thing it would be difficult to argue, but—Barbara had escaped. Barbara almost certainly knew where Lessing was, and would go straight to him. Loyalty or not, the risk to her was real.

"Yes," Rollison answered.

"Why?"

"It's his flat; Lessing was a kind of unofficial subtenant. It's his cottage, too; Lessing had the use of it whenever Carruthers didn't need it. Carruthers isn't like Lessing in appearance, but there are superficial likenesses, in height, build, complexion and colour of hair. The two men might be mistaken for each other if only descriptions were used as a guide."

"Is Carruthers a personal friend of yours, too?"

"No. An acquaintance whom I met through Lessing, some years ago."

"How did you meet Mr. Lorne and his daughter, Mr. Rollison?" The politeness was over-insistent, and was why Rollison found this office, the interview, everything about the Yard so strange. There seemed a kind of hidden menace, as if at a given moment Ellerby would come out with some devastating accusation.

"Lorne and I have served on a number of charity committees for years, and I liked him," Rollison answered. "He wanted me to introduce his daughter to friends of mine, and I did."

"Was this a matter of professional introductions to a certain level of society to which Mr. Lorne could not aspire on his own?" asked Ellerby softly.

Rollison grinned.

"It was not! I may take money for what you would call dabbling in crime when it should be left to the police, but I only introduce friends to my friends. I like Lorne and his daughter."

"These demands, of ten different lots of a thousand pounds, Mr. Rollison—is it true that you advised Lorne to send ten per cent of the sum demanded to each of the addresses given to him?"

So Lorne had been absolutely ruthless, telling the police everything, so determined was he to make sure that nothing that might help his daughter was left unsaid.

"Yes," answered Rollison.

Ellerby had an unexpectedly broad smile, and very white teeth. He showed them now.

"Damned good idea," he said, "and I've asked Mr. Lorne to do it, in spite of the way the news has broken. It's just possible that each one of the lots of money will be collected. Each address will be watched from tomorrow morning onwards, and if that packet is collected the collector will be followed. I know, I know, it isn't likely that the blackmailer will expect anything now that the news has been broadcast, but it's worth trying, I think."

Rollison shrugged. "It can't do any harm. The addresses all looked like calling addresses to me. Were they?"

"Yes, shops which act as *poste restante*. Not much which misses you," went on Ellerby, almost exuberantly. "If I'm not careful I shall begin to believe that your reputation is justified! Mr. Rollison, we've gone pretty deeply into this, as you can imagine. We would like to consult the Sûreté Nationale, and in fact we have asked them to look out for Major Lessing at the Channel ports and the airfields serving northern France and Paris. We'd like them to watch Major Carruthers' *appartement*, in case Lessing goes there, but we haven't yet a case strong enough to go that far. Paris would do it, but until there is a warrant out for Major Lessing, my superiors don't want the French police to be too deeply involved. At the moment we want Major Lessing for questioning. I've asked for a warrant for his arrest, but there are difficulties—it may take us twenty-four hours to get it. If you go to Paris you'll be on your own. The French police won't take the same casual view that we do of the amateur. If you run into trouble there you will really be in trouble."

Rollison felt his heart pounding, this time with excitement based on the belief that they were not going to stop him from taking that aircraft.

"I'll take the risk," he said. "Do you know that Miss Lorne can pilot a plane, and that her father has a private one?"

"We know more," said Ellerby. "Lorne's daughter took off in it, a little while before I came in, that's why I had to keep you waiting. All the papers were in order, she had her new passport—she went to her home and collected it. She is behaving now with quite remarkable clear-sightedness, Mr. Rollison, not like a sorely frightened bride who might have been deceived."

"She's in love with Lessing," Rollison said, and added heavily: "So she did go to Paris."

"Do you know if she knows Carruthers?"

"I'm not sure."

Ellerby said, "I don't know any way you can be sure of getting to Paris ahead of her, Mr. Rollison, but I do know that there is a vacant seat on the two-o'clock aircraft, B.E.A., and you've just time to catch it."

It was then twenty to one; there was comfortable time for Rollison to go to his flat, collect his passport and some money, and drive to the London Airport. There was plenty of time to sit and look into the Scotland Yard man's eyes and then to ask quietly:

"May I take an automatic pistol?"

"You'll have to take your chance with the French Customs, ours won't stop you."

Rollison stood up.

"Thanks. But why all this?"

Ellerby spread his hands. "It's very simple, Mr. Rollison. Ever since I can remember, you've been acting in a way most of us have thought unjustified. We're trained specialists, and you've been the interfering amateur. Bill Grice always told me that I was wrong, that you see and can tackle angles which we can't, and can take chances that we can't. He was the only senior officer here who believed in giving you your head, Mr. Rollison. I can see why now. Certainly you can go to Paris and do things that we can't. The quicker this business is settled, the better I'll like it, and I don't give a damn whether you settle it, we do or the French police do. I do care whether that young woman lives or dies, and I think she might be going straight to her death. But I've nothing to go on that will enable me to ask the French police to co-operate, yet."

After a pause, Rollison said, "Now I know for certain."

"Know what for certain?" asked Ellerby.

"That I like policemen," answered Rollison, when he was half-way to the door.

17

UNEXPECTED GUEST

ROLLISON did not go into details, but simply told Jolly that the police were playing the game his way, and sent his man to get his passport, a store of French francs which was always kept at the flat and some traveller's cheques also kept for emergency; and Jolly packed an overnight bag. Jolly tried to hurry, but could not; yet when the bag was packed and Rollison ready to go, he said :

"May I drive you, sir?"

"No," said Rollison. "There's far too much to do here." In fact, Jolly needed rest. "Get all that Fleet Street business done first."

"I've attended to it, sir."

"Make a nuisance of yourself, and do it again. Then check everything you can about Carruthers on this side, find out whether he had any reason to dislike Major Lessing—all that and as much more as you can think up. Try to find out more about Holy Joe, who he is and what he does for Carruthers. And finally——"

Rollison hesitated.

"Yes, sir?" Jolly was eager.

"The police have allowed—in fact encouraged—Mr. Lorne to send out those hundred-pound baits," Rollison told him. "I'd like to know if they get any results from watching the addresses and seeing who collects. I've a feeling that the blackmail might be an outsize red-herring to distract attention from the real motive. I'd also like to know why Mr. Lorne is prepared to go on with it. The threat of disclosing the marriage to Helen Goodman doesn't serve

now, so—has there been another threat, of another kind?
Is he under different pressure? If so, what?"

"I'll see if I can find out anything, sir," Jolly promised.

Rollison went out and hurried down the stairs; he could
hurry in comfort provided he kept his head straight and
went on his toes, so as not to jolt his neck. He had seen no
police or detectives when he had returned from the Yard,
except the man who had driven him, and he saw none now.
The centre of the case had shifted, and Ellerby could not
have signalled his intention to work with him more clearly;
unless he was being very cunning.

He might be pretending this friendly willingness to work
together so as to disarm Rollison.

He might be watching him much less ostentatiously.

Rollison dumped his overnight case in the back seat and
took the wheel. He drove sedately towards Piccadilly, then
towards Hyde Park Corner, heading for Putney, Hammer-
smith, the Great West Road and the Airport. He was near
the Lyric Theatre when he suspected that one of the tyres
was low, but he did not slow down; they were tubeless, and
should keep up for as long as he needed the car. He felt
the bumpiness of a stretch of road more markedly, and felt
a little anxious; the last thing he wanted to do was to change
a tyre. The clock on the fascia board showed that it was
twenty minutes past one; he had ample time, provided he
did not have to throw too much away.

The tyre would have to last as far as the airport.

He felt it, bumpety-bumpety-bump when he was near
Turnham Green. There were garages along here, and surely
one where he could get a taxi to take him to the airport, if
the driver would get a move on.

He saw two garages along on the right, and pulled into
the kerb opposite them; that saved the need for crossing
the stream of traffic coming towards him. No one was in
sight at the garage. He got out of the car and looked at
the two front tyres; they were perfectly all right. He went
to the back, and saw that the offside tyre was nearly flat;

and then he saw that the valve was in an odd position; it had been badly wrenched out of its seating, and undoubtedly the puncture was there.

It was twenty-five minutes past one, and if he could get away from here in five minutes he would catch the aircraft. He stepped into the road behind the car, and as he did so, heard a sound at the boot lid. He looked round and saw it opening. Startled, he backed away hastily as it was flung open.

He looked into a man's face; the face of a small man, a complete stranger, who was crouching inside the big boot.

Minutes counted.

If Rollison spent any time dealing with this man he might miss that two-o'clock aircraft; and Ellerby would not have thought it worth sending him in a hurry unless he had believed there was real danger to Barbara.

He heard a car horn, wailing.

The little man just crouched there, defiantly, as if daring him to raise an alarm.

Minutes counted.

A car came up behind him, moving at such a speed that Rollison spun round, to jump out of the way. Traffic was too thick for him to jump into the road, so he stepped smartly back on to the pavement. The car was a dark-green Jaguar. Its nearside door opened and a man jumped out and came hurrying to him.

"That's enough," the newcomer said abruptly. "You've had it."

There was the crouching man, staring up at him; this man, big and hefty; and the driver, also getting out. It all happened in a second or two, and he was still incapable of sudden movement.

"Don't know how you thought you could get away with it," the speaker went on, and gripped Rollison's forearm, while the little man moved quickly out of the boot and slammed it. The driver of the Jaguar came up, and Rollison was surrounded on three sides. "Why don't you use your mind?" the speaker asked in a clear voice. "It's no use knocking off a Rolls-Bentley."

A man and woman, passing, looked round.

It was a thousand to one that these men weren't police. They were here to stop him from getting to the airport, so he was not wanted in Paris. The need to cross the Channel became a screeching urgency.

"Fetch a copper, Andy," the speaker went on, and the little man began to move away promptly; the act was brilliantly convincing. A group of seven or eight people had gathered, and the speaker still held Rollison's arm tightly, as he continued :

"We've had a lot of trouble with car thieves lately, so Andy makes a habit of getting in the boot. Your number was up before you started."

"Ah," said Rollison, as if owlishly.

Even if he made a run for it he would not be able to catch that aircraft now; the men had succeeded. No policeman was in sight, and "Andy" would not bring one. They would waste ten minutes or so; and they might even have laid everything on well enough to have a stage policeman in the offing.

He could argue; he might even persuade the crowd; but he could not get on board that aircraft, unless a miracle happened, and there was no sign of a miracle. Inwardly he was seething, outwardly he showed no sign of anger or disappointment.

Andy was out of sight.

"You haven't much to say for yourself," said the man who was holding Rollison.

"No," said Rollison. "I haven't recovered from being accused of stealing my own car."

"That's a good one!" The man guffawed; while Rollison's thoughts were racing to hopes of chartering a special plane. If the others were so anxious to stop him from catching that particular plane it could only mean that the next hour or two was vital. "You wait until the police arrive, then we'll see whose car it is. Where's Andy, Tim?"

The other man said, "Dunno."

Seconds counted.

Then the miracle happened.

A car drew up alongside the Jaguar, a small Austin— with Jolly at the wheel.

.   .   .   .   .   .

Jolly looked peaky and pale, but his eyes were very bright as he opened the door of the Austin and got out. A huge lorry pulled up behind him, the driver hooted; and a dozen cars were slowing down behind the lorry, but Jolly took no notice at all. The two men holding Rollison looked at Jolly in surprise, and he glanced at them as he said almost meekly:

"I thought there might be an attempt to stop you, sir, so I followed as soon as I could. Can I be of any assistance?"

"Who the hell are you?" the spokesman demanded, and the crowd now stared at Jolly, so obviously a gentleman's gentleman, so neat, small, elderly, prim and proper.

"I am Mr. Rollison's butler," Jolly announced, with great dignity. Then he doubled his right fist and drove it into the nearer man's stomach. Rollison bent his elbow and rammed it against the other man's ribs, making him drop his hold and stagger back. "*Quickly, sir,*" Jolly breathed, and the next moment Rollison was squeezing into the Austin; its engine was still running. The huge lorry had come too close to get past, a line of traffic behind the Austin was now a hundred yards long, and from afar off two real policemen were coming but not hurrying. Jolly slammed the door. Someone on the pavement shouted and darted forward, but Rollison let in the clutch and put the car in gear and shot off. The wail of the lorry's horn was loud in his ears. The road ahead was clear as far as he could see, and within seconds he was travelling at forty-five miles an hour; not

far ahead, on the Great West Road, he could do what speed
he liked. Jolly would make sure that the police did not send
out a call for him, he need not worry about that.

Need he?

He reached the Great West Road and put his foot down;
the little car's speedometer needle swung towards the eighty
mark, and quivered on it. He flashed past car after car,
leaving even a Rolls-Bentley standing. Nothing was on the
road behind him, so no one was giving chase.

He still had twenty-seven minutes.

.   .   .   .   .

He had seven minutes when he swung off the road into
the airport enclosure, and he knew the airport road so well
that he did not have to stop and inquire the way. He went
beneath the underpass and swung towards the Queen's
Building, the passenger and the loading bays; and he
reached the spot where he was due with three minutes to
spare. Porters were waiting. He jumped out, and a porter
said:

"Paris, sir?"

"Yes."

"Flight 71, sir. Shall I take your luggage?"

It was on the seat of the Rolls-Bentley.

"Left my case behind," Rollison said, "but I've a passport and ticket. Can you get someone to park my car, my
man will be here for it soon."

"Okay," the porter said. "This way, sir. You'll just about
do it."

He would do it with seconds to spare.

Everyone was eager to help; Customs and Immigration
raised no difficulties, it was almost as if the police had
smoothed a path for him. Officials hustled him out to the
field. The aircraft was already warming up, and the rest
of the passengers were aboard. Rollison saw mechanics and
ground staff waiting to take the steps and the chocks away,
and every passenger seemed to be staring, as if accusing

him of making them late. Now that he was climbing the steps he felt worse than he had all day; after last night's blows on the head he was in no shape for this : he hadn't been in shape for the emergency at all.

Thank God for Jolly !

A stewardess beamed at him.

"All right, sir ?"

"Thanks, yes. I don't deserve to get to Paris, do I ?"

"You've half a minute yet, sir." She was gay, he was gay, but he wanted to sit down. She escorted him to a seat on the corridor side, but with a position from which there would be a fair view. The doors were pushed to. He heard the throbbing and felt the vibration of the aircraft, and it was almost soothing. He hardly seemed to sit down before the plane began to taxi for position before moving towards the runway.

In a little over an hour they would touch down at the Paris Airport.

There was nothing he could do until he got there; very little useful purpose would be served even by thinking about the issues, although Lessing's friend Carruthers and the hairy Holy Joe were vivid in his mind; almost as vivid as Barbara, for whom he was afraid. He closed his eyes, and felt the engines give the final roar before the take-off; the one moment in a flight when he always felt uneasy. When he opened his eyes the land was sweeping past, and the machine was bumping and vibrating; and then suddenly it was still, as if it were floating.

It was.

That thought made him grin.

Then he saw Robert Lorne, staring round from a seat four places in front of him.

18

PARIS

IT was impossible to mistake Barbara's father; that round face and the round head, the perfectly fitting coat; and, just now, the angry, hostile expression in his pale eyes. He did not get up. The earth seemed to be swaying past Rollison's eyes as the aircraft banked a little. He hardly noticed it. He was thrust against the safety belt, and had no doubt that Lorne was held tight in by his round fat belly; that was why he was twisting round in such an odd way.

Rollison raised a hand, to acknowledge him.

Lorne turned away and disappeared behind his seat.

Rollison thought, "I don't even get time to think."

Why was Barbara's father here, on the way to Paris? Did he know where his daughter was likely to go? Had he any reason to think that Lessing was in Paris?

One thing was certain : it could not be coincidence.

First, the three men trying to stop him; and now this.

He watched the houses and the fields, tiny patches in a toy country, as they became smaller and smaller beneath the aircraft. The momentary tension of the take-off had gone. The stewardess was coming round with a dish of barley sugar, and the :

FASTEN BELTS
NO SMOKING

sign flashed off at the end of the cabin.

Passengers were beginning to talk. The man sitting next to Rollison turned his head and said, "Well, that was smooth enough."

"Perfect," agreed Rollison and took out cigarettes. The

other did not smoke. Rollison drew on a cigarette, and leaned back, trying to get all the morning's happenings into the proper perspective. The basic need, to find Guy Lessing and to prove what he had done, had not changed; but there were many new factors. Barbara, with what seemed to be a flash of recollection for the second time in two days. Lorne's attitude. The bitterness between father and daughter over Lessing, which must have gone very deep indeed. The decision of the Yard to let him, Rollison, have his head— which they certainly would not have done had they felt capable of handling this situation for themselves. Undoubtedly it was the French angle which gave them trouble.

How had Lorne discovered where Barbara was going? Was he under some kind of pressure which Rollison knew nothing about?

Was it even conceivable that he would try to keep Barbara away from Lessing by force?

There was another fact : if Barbara and her father knew about the Paris association with this affair, and knew where to go, it meant that they had known about it before to-day.

Did it?

There was a possibility that one of the newspapers had discovered that Mrs. Lessing the Second had just arrived from Paris, but would that in itself send Barbara and her father here?

The aircraft was very high, was not quivering very much and the noise of the engines were subdued. Newspapers were rustling, magazines opening, a small child ran down the gangway between the seats. The next moment of tension would be on landing at Orly.

It was as perfect a landing as it had been a take-off.

Rollison was third off the aircraft, and he did not turn round to see Lorne; he could catch up with Lorne when they were through Customs. He was very conscious of the weight of an automatic pistol against his side as he stood in front of a thin-faced, middle-aged Customs officer, who found it hard to believe that he had no luggage, not even a briefcase. In fluent French, Rollison explained that he had left everything at the London airport. There were smiles, gestures, *bon voyage, m'sieu* !

Rollison stepped out of the Customs buildings into bright sunshine, fierce heat and the roaring of engines warming up. There was a sign : *taxis*. He waited back until three, all vintage ones, had been taken, and took the fourth, a sleek-looking modern Citroen with the sloping roof. Lorne was still at the Customs.

"Yes, sir, I will wait, I have all day," the taxi-man said, as Rollison slipped a five-thousand-franc note into his hand. He was small and perky, with waxed moustaches. Rollison sat in the back, still very much on edge, looking out of the window for Lorne. He wanted to make sure where Lorne went; he was desperately anxious to get to the French address where he might find Lessing, Barbara or at least Carruthers. The address had burned itself into his mind : 79, Rue de Gaspin, Paris, 6e. That was off the Boulevard St. Germain, or thereabouts. He knew the area slightly; a few years ago it had been the centre of the arts and painting fashion, but that had shifted lately.

Lorne came hurrying.

A big American car, a dual-tone Chrysler, was waiting with a chauffeur not far away. Lorne headed straight for it. The chauffeur got out, and Rollison said to his driver :

"Start off now. We want to keep that Chrysler in sight. Can you do it?"

"With this motor there is nothing I cannot do," declared the Frenchman. He winked. "Besides, it is smaller, so in the traffic it is easier."

"Prove it," challenged Rollison.

The man gave a confident laugh as he started off. They passed the Chrysler, and the sun glinted on its red and pale-green cellulose. Sitting so that he could not easily be seen, Rollison saw Lorne handed in by the chauffeur, who looked hot if immaculate. Soon, the taxi was leading the way in a stream of airfield traffic, towards the main road; and once the Chrysler had turned towards Paris, the taxi-driver put his foot down, and left every other car on the road standing; except the Chrysler.

The taxi-driver now crouched over his wheel. From time to time Rollison caught a glimpse of his bright eyes in the driving-mirror; and from the other's tension, he judged that this was not going to be so easy as he had thought. He looked round. The Chrysler was perhaps half a mile behind, and there was only slow-moving traffic between them. It seemed to be sweeping forward.

"He'll never do it," Rollison thought.

The Citroen's speedometer needle was quivering around the 150 kilometres mark, but the only real hope was that traffic would slow the Chrysler down. It came sweeping on, and now Rollison could almost see the whites of the chauffeur's eyes. He could not see Lorne.

The Chrysler swept past.

"It is possessed of the devil, that one," the taxi-driver growled, and it would be easy to believe that there were tears of vexation in his eyes. "Have I got wings?"

"Keep going," Rollison said. "Traffic might slow him down."

"Not that one," the driver said gloomily. "He will jump over the top of the traffic." He settled down, and the needle still quivered about the hundred and fifty, until traffic lights, traffic gendarmes and the thickening traffic of the outer suburbs of Paris slowed them down.

"Where is it you wish to go?" the taxi-driver asked glumly.

"79, Rue de Gaspin."

"*Si, m'sieu.*"

Now the driver was determined to prove his prowess, and he wove in and out of the traffic like a crazed thing; and no one seemed surprised. He crossed the river near the Place de la Concorde, and soon they were on the Boulevard St. Germain, swinging along it as if this were the open

country road; no one stopped them. Motor scooters swerved
towards them and swung away, as if at the mercy of the
wind. Green one-decker buses snarled, snorted at them and
stuck out their wagging indicators, but the driver swept past.
Near St. Germain de Prés, he turned left, cutting in front
of an approaching wine truck, whose driver leaned out and
swore at him with masterly abandon. They flashed by
antique shops and picture galleries, and then swung right,
then left and found themselves in a street so narrow that
parked cars were pulled up half on the cobbled road and half
on the flagstones of the pavement.

The taxi-driver's eyes brightened.

"*Voilà, m'sieu!*"

"Magnificent," praised Rollison. "Will you go to the end
of the street, and be ready for me when I come out? I may
be in a hurry again."

"I shall be waiting," the driver promised.

Rollison got out, and stared up at the tiny balconies at
two floors, and all the shuttered windows; not a single one
was unshuttered, not for the first time he marvelled at the
way the French liked to shut out the light of day.

Number 79 was like all the rest of the houses here; dirty,
drab, in need not only of painting but also of much plaster.
A little way along a bedraggled tricolour, relic from some
day of celebration, drooped in the heat which seemed to rise
up from the cobbles. There was a huge wooden doorway
with a smaller door set in it. Rollison opened the smaller
door and stepped into a cobbled courtyard, where an old
palm-tree wilted in a tub and a line of washing, drab and
bedraggled, hung across one corner. A thin tabby cat
stalked across in front of Rollison.

The entrance to the house was on the right, and Rollison
stepped inside. He heard nothing. There was no concierge,
only a little empty room, now used to store old boxes, newspapers and bottles. A circular staircase rose above his head,
narrow and dilapidated, as if it had been built and beautifully decorated in gilt and pale blue in the days of Louis

Quinze, and not been touched since. Rollison went up. At the first landing there was a card which must have been pinned to the shabby-looking wood for years. It announced M. Panier; there was only one flat at each landing.

Still Rollison heard no sound.

He seemed to be drawn on by some compulsive force. The silence seemed a threat in itself. Neither the chauffeur nor Lorne had been down in the street, so there was a chance that each of them was up here. Had Lorne come to take his daughter away by sheer physical force?

The stone steps made little sound under his own footsteps. He reached the next landing, looked up into the narrow well of the staircase and saw that there were at least two more. There was no card at the second door. Rollison hesitated, then went up the next flight and saw the card he wanted to see: a card yellow and dusty, curling at each corner, and reading: *Major Ralph Carruthers*.

Rollison bent down.

There was no letter-box, only an iron knocker and an iron bell-push, but he first looked at blankness through the keyhole, and then put his ear to it. For the first time since he had come here, he heard a sound; and he did not like it, for it was like a moan.

He drew back.

He could just hear it now.

He tried the handle of the door, but although it turned, the door would not open. It was an old-fashioned lock of the safest kind known fifty years ago, but unless the door was bolted, he should be able to get the door open as quickly as he had the front door of the mews flat in Heddle Mews. He took out his skeleton key, and as he did so, heard a sound below him. He stood very still, the key in his hand; and then heard a bell ring. A moment later a door opened, then closed.

Rollison started to work.

It took him longer than he had expected, for the lock was much more intricate than he had judged. He kept working. There was a possibility that this was a special lock, made to look old-fashioned. He began to wonder whether it would be better to go downstairs again and climb up to the apartment by the balconies and windows facing the courtyard, but he kept working; the metallic sounds were very clear.

This was the third time he had forced entry. At the cottage the door had been open, at the mews he had forced a door like this; each time he had got in, to find himself face to face with death.

That moaning seemed louder.

He felt the key grip, twisted very slowly and gingerly, and heard the lock click back. He waited for fully thirty seconds, to make sure that no one had heard, then turned the handle and pushed the door.

It opened.

The moaning sound, although not really loud, was much more distinct now.

Fear that it was Barbara was deep within him.

He stepped into a narrow passage, with tall doors on three sides; only one of them was ajar. He went towards this, and seemed to hear rustling sounds all about him. Twice he had done this, twice he had stepped into death, twice some man had been lurking in wait for him, once to strike him down, once to strike at Jolly.

The moaning was coming from the room with the open door.

Rollison flung the door back, so that it would smack against any man hiding behind it, but it banged against the wall. He stepped into a tall, spacious room, a drawing-room. A man lay on the floor beside the ornate fireplace, and at the foot of an old-fashioned, shabby brocaded chair.

It was almost an anti-climax, for this was the chauffeur who had been waiting for Lorne.

Rollison saw him twisting his head from side to side.

He stepped out of this room and approached each of the others, even more fearful of what he might find; but he found nothing. There were five rooms in the *appartement*, a bathroom which looked as if it was the first ever known in Paris, and a kitchen. There was a lived-in look about every room, and one big double bed was not made from the previous morning; but no one else was here.

Rollison went back to the little passage-like hallway, and the front door.

Why attack Lorne's chauffeur?

Why leave him here?

He heard a creak of sound, and a faint moaning again, from the drawing-room; and it was the combination of noises which thrust himself into a realisation of the trap which he had nearly walked into once again. He passed the open door of the drawing-room, glancing in as he did so. The chauffeur lay in almost the same position, but had moved his legs. Rollison turned round, and went in. He saw the man's eyes flicker, and felt quite sure what was going to happen. He bent down, and put out a hand as if for the other's wrist and pulse, and with a swift, convulsive heave the man lunged at him, snatching at his arm, intending to bring him crashing down; but for that moment of understanding, he would have succeeded.

Rollison swayed to one side, shot out his right hand, gripped the other's wrist and twisted so savagely that he brought a gasp of genuine pain.

Then the man pulled himself free.

19

SEARCH

THE chauffeur was big and powerful, and had recovered from the moment of surprise. Rollison's left hand was almost useless, and the stiffness at his neck prevented him from moving freely. If this developed into a fight he would have no chance at all; he had to end it swiftly. He grabbed the other's right wrist again, before the man could straighten up, twisted and thrust it upwards. This hold was so tight that if the man struggled, he would break his arm.

Did he realise that?

Rollison felt the powerful resistance of the muscular body. He sensed that the man was trying to bring his left arm into action, and could not secure that with his own good hand; this was the moment of decision.

He said in French, "If you don't stop, I'll break your arm."

The man seemed as if he would take the chance, then suddenly relaxed, as if submitting. Rollison did not trust him any more than he would have trusted Lorne, and kept his hold very tight.

"I can still break it," he said, still in French.

"I know." That came in English which had a Cockney twang. There was sweat on the chauffeur's forehead and on his upper lip; now he was really in pain.

"Then don't tempt me," Rollison warned. He chose his moment, and thrust a little harder until it was obvious to the other that his bone was going to snap; then Rollison let go, backed away and, as he went, slipped his automatic from his pocket. He went to a chair just behind him, felt it

with the back of his knees and sat down. "And don't make
any mistake, I'll gladly use this. Where is Lorne?"

The answer came pat.

"I don't know."

"You'd better remember."

"I don't know," the chauffeur repeated roughly. "I can't
tell you a thing."

"Who was here when you arrived?"

"Miss Barbara."

"Alone?"

"Yes."

"What happened?"

"Mr. Lorne took her away."

"The last time I saw her she wasn't in a mood to be taken
away by anyone."

"You don't know the man," the chauffeur said. "When
he wants a thing he gets it. He had a hypodermic syringe
all ready, with knock-out drops in it. She was asleep on her
feet within minutes."

"Where did he take her?"

"I don't *know*."

"If she was unconscious she had to be carried, and he
couldn't carry her far."

"I carried her down to the car," the chauffeur said.

He wasn't scared in the sense that many people would
be; possibly he did not think that the threat from the automatic was very real. He sat on the floor, staring with a kind
of impertinence which was not far removed from insolence,
and he seemed to say, "Maybe I'm lying, but what can you
do about it?"

"Where did you take her?"

"I put her in the back seat of the Chrysler. Lorne said he
was going to drive her away."

"Where to?"

"I don't know."

"Has he an *appartement* in Paris?"

"For all I know, he has dozens."

"Don't you work for him?"

"I'm from a hire agency, and he paid me in hard cash to fix you."

That might be true.

Rollison felt as he had felt often in this affair: a sense of frustration and almost of anti-climax. If Lorne had called a man from a hire agency, then obviously the man was not likely to know where he could be found. Short of using physical torture, there was no way to make sure that the chauffeur was telling the truth; but Rollison had a feeling that he was.

Rollison said, "Take out your wallet, and toss it across to me. Don't try to be clever."

The chauffeur put his hand to his pocket, took out his wallet and slid it across the floor; it stopped a yard in front of Rollison, as undoubtedly the man had intended. Rollison stood up, kept the other covered, bent down and retrieved it; the odd thing was that he did not really think that the chauffeur was going to attack him. He shook the contents of the wallet out, and among them were half a dozen cards, all saying the same thing :

Anglo-American Car Rentals
English and American Chauffeur-Guides.
Offices throughout Paris.

The man was grinning.

"Satisfied?"

"What did Lorne tell you to do with me?"

"He said I was to knock the daylight out of you, and then lock you in one of these cupboards. He said you'd been more nuisance than you were worth, and he had to get you out of the way."

"Ah," said Rollison. "His trouble was the poor quality of his helpers. How much did he pay you?"

"A hundred thousand francs."

Nearly a hundred pounds, thought Rollison; and that added up. Lorne had turned right against him, whatever

the reason, and when that reason was known, Rollison
believed that he would understand a great deal more of
what had happened.

He could keep asking questions, but did not think this
man knew a great deal. He stood up, and the other began
to get to his feet at the same time, grinning, as if he now
believed that Rollison had thrown his chance away.

"You wouldn't use that gun in a thousand years," he
said, "you might as well put it in your pocket."

He strode forward.

Rollison pressed the trigger, with the gun pointing into
the man's face. He saw the moment of dread which showed
in the dark-blue eyes. A cloud of vapour billowed out, and
as it came, relief replaced the dread; but the chauffeur
could do nothing to help himself. He began to back away,
hands at his face, tears already streaming down his cheeks.
He was quite helpless as Rollison took his right arm, held it
behind him in a hammer lock and hustled him towards one
of the big cupboards; there were a few coats and oddments
hanging up, but there was plenty of room for the chauffeur.

Rollison pushed him in, and locked the door; that lock
would take a lot of forcing. He pushed a sofa towards the
cupboard, and lodged it against the double doors. Then he
moved away, sweating a little, but satisfied that he had
won both time and a chance.

He began to search the apartment.

Obviously, two people lived here; there were a man's
clothes, a tall man's, almost certainly Carruthers'. A few
garments were French, but most were British made. The
woman's clothes seemed likely to fit the dead woman of the
mews flat, but that was guesswork.

He found letters addressed to Carruthers, but none to
Lessing.

He found a letter from Lessing, asking if the cottage at
Bane was likely to be free—and the period mentioned was
this very week; this was the letter which Lessing had sent
to ask for the cottage honeymoon. There was a small room

overlooking the courtyard at one end of a long passage, a
dressing-room, with a wardrobe and dressing-table. Rollison
opened a drawer almost perfunctorily, and saw a box of
grease-paint, and several plastic bags.

"Well, well," he breathed, and opened a bag and shook
out the contents : a beard and moustache, beautifully made,
and very like Holy Joe's.

· · · · ·

Holy Joe's beard could have been false, there was no
doubt of that. Was he Carruthers in a different guise ?

· · · · ·

Rollison left his discovery, and finished searching writing-
cabinets, drawers, cupboards, every place where papers
might be hidden, but discovered nothing else at all. Judging
from what he saw here, this was Carruthers' flat, he lived
a normal life here, presumably with his wife, perhaps with
a mistress; and certainly with the make-up.

Rollison spent an hour going from room to room, looking
everywhere, listening now and again in case anyone was
approaching, but he found and heard nothing until, towards the end of the abortive search, the chauffeur began to
bang on the door. Rollison ignored him.

He could wait here for Carruthers, if Carruthers was
coming back, but could not expect to find Barbara. Lessing might come here, but there was nothing to indicate
that he had been yet. Every lead seemed to take Rollison
away from the main problem, it was as if he was the centre
of a fantastic hoax, but—those two dead women hadn't
been part of a hoax.

He went to the telephone, in the passageway, and ran
his finger down the L's. There was no telephone number
under the L's. There was no telephone number under the
name of Lorne.

Then he heard footsteps on the stairs; of a man, hurrying.
This was a big man who came with firm tread; an

athletic type. He might not be coming to this *appartement*; but as he reached the landing, he slowed down. Next moment there was a scraping sound, as of a key in the lock of the door. Rollison stepped into the drawing-room. The chauffeur had given up banging for the time being.

The front door opened.

Rollison, staring between the crack between this door and the frame, saw Major Ralph Carruthers come in. Carruthers certainly had that superficial likeness to Lessing, but that was all; no one who knew Lessing could mistake this man for him. He was of a height with Holy Joe, but Rollison couldn't be sure that it was the same man; he hadn't seen Holy Joe often or clearly enough.

Carruthers was not smiling, but looked quite relaxed; he was whistling softly, a little old-fashioned tune. Rollison thought that he was coming into this room, but he changed his mind and went into one of the others : the bedroom.

His whistling was louder.

Then the telephone bell rang.

It startled Rollison, who moved into a corner, so that there was no chance of being seen. Carruthers came striding out, a man who was obviously physically fit, and at that moment gave an impression of energy held on a leash; in other words a typical Guards officer.

" 'Allo ?" On the telephone he sounded like any Frenchman; but next moment there was a change in his manner, a kind of stiffening, and he spoke in English. "Hallo, Guy," he said, "what are you doing over here ?"

There was a long pause. Then :

"No, I haven't seen an English newspaper for weeks, you get out of the habit . . .

"What kind of trouble ?

"Well, yes, of course, you're always welcome here, but I don't want serious trouble, old chap, you know how the French authorities are about foreigners. We're allowed plenty of rope provided we live peacefully and lawfully, but once they think we're a bit risky, they shoot us back home. I don't want to come home."

There was a longer pause.

"No, Guy, I'm not being unhelpful, but I'm just telling you the simple truth. I don't want to get myself involved in anything which concerns the police, and you sound as if you really are in trouble with them."

This time, he paused only for a moment.

"I tell you what," he said. "Let's meet outside for a Pernod, the cafés are empty at this time of day, and we can talk quite freely. Then you can tell me what it's all about. . . . Where are you now? . . . Well, allow half an hour to get to St. Germain de Prés, and let's say the Brasserie Lippe. If it is more crowded than I expect, we can go somewhere else."

"Of course I want to help, Guy."

He rang off.

For some time, it seemed an age to Rollison, Carruthers stood very still by the telephone. Then he turned away and went back to the room he had come from. He was no longer whistling. Rollison could not hear him—nor could he hear the man in the cupboard. He wheeled the upturned sofa away and unlocked the door. The chauffeur was leaning back against the wall—just coming round. Rollison gave him another whiff of the gas, closed and locked the cupboard door, and then went to the passage-way.

Carruthers was making no sound.

Rollison opened the front door, stepped on to the landing and closed the door very quietly; yet there was a slight click, which Carruthers might hear. He pressed the bell, and it rang very loudly. He smoothed down his hair as he waited, and shrugged his coat into position.

Carruthers opened the door.

"Good afternoon," he said, and then thrust his face forward, recognised Rollison and went on, "Good lord, it's Rollison! Come in." He stood aside, and then pushed open the door of the drawing-room. "What on earth brings you here? I suppose I really needn't ask," he went on, before Rollison could answer. "Guy Lessing's just been on the telephone to say that he's in a spot of bother, and I gather he's on the run from the police at home. That why you're here?"

"Yes."

"Guy always was lucky in his friends," said Carruthers, but there was a touch of bitterness in his voice. "Well, take a pew. Anything I can get you in the way of a drink, or is it too early for you confirmed Englishmen? . . . I thought so. Well, have a cigarette, if you can stand these French gaspers. If you've come to hear how inevitable it was that Guy should run into trouble, you've come to the right man."

20

ABOUT GUY LESSING . . .

"I MUST have known Guy as long as you have," Carruthers went on, very slowly. "We lived near each other as boys, the families were friends. True I didn't go to school with him, like you did, and he went to Oxford, but we were in the Army together. Fourteen years. You get to know a man in the Army."

"Yes," Rollison agreed.

"There never was a braver man than Guy, and he was a damned good soldier," said Carruthers. "At times I almost envied him." He grinned unexpectedly. "If you know what I mean! He got instant obedience all the time, you could sense that the men idolised him, but they thought that I was just another b.f. who didn't know half as much about soldiering as they did. You can always tell. The life suited me, though, although it got pretty sticky towards the end, and I wasn't sorry when I was axed. I think Guy was—he would have liked to have died on his feet, even after being wounded."

Carruthers paused.

He was a better-looking man than Lessing, his eyes were vivid blue—Holy Joe's had been, too—and he had fuller lips; it was a strong, handsome face, and there was something very human about it; people would like Carruthers just as they would be inclined to be wary of Lessing. Carruthers lacked Lessing's aloofness, and had a natural ease of manner. Yet to the men serving under them, it had been the other way round.

Carruthers was sitting back in an old-fashioned armchair, holding a cigarette but not smoking it. He looked very alert, and very thoughtful.

"I'm telling you this because I know you're a close friend of Guy's," he went on. "Wild horses wouldn't drag it out of me otherwise. The thing is to try to help him. And the devil of it is, everything began after he was discharged from hospital. He was there for six months, remember."

"I remember," Rollison said.

"He seemed fine at first, and I didn't notice anything different," Carruthers went on. "Then he began to do odd things. The first I noticed was when he went off with my current girl." Carruthers gave a queer, twisted grin. "Fair competition and all that, but in general friend doesn't poach on friend. We were in Paris. I needn't go into details, but there was a little charmer who really knew her way about town, and I think I might have married her. Guy swept her off her feet. That's the odd thing about Guy: he could always sweep a girl off her feet, although a lot of men think him a cold fish. I took it a bit hard, until he turned up a couple of weeks later, and—believe it or not—didn't know a thing about it. At first I thought he was just being smart. I wanted to row with him, but he wouldn't, just insisted that he didn't know what I was talking about. And I'm sure he didn't."

Rollison felt very cold in this shadowy room, with the sun shining in bright bars against the shutters outside.

"Other things happened, and it was obvious that one half of his mind didn't know what the other half was doing. He was once nearly in jug for a couple of thousand pounds —I covered up for him. But his chief trouble was with the pretties. Before the injury he had never been what you might call a ladies' man, but he became a positive Don Juan. Believe it or not, whenever he was challenged, he said he didn't know what I was talking about. Damned queer business altogether. I talked to Dave Willard—you know Dr. Willard."

"Yes." Rollison's voice was very quiet.

"Dave was a bit shaken, but finally agreed that it was a case of split personality. He seemed to think that it was

latent all the time—I suppose it is in most of us—and that
the wound had brought it out. With anyone else, I would
have called enough enough, but boyhood friends and all
that. There was nothing spiteful or harmful as far as I could
see, apart from his recklessness with money. That had to
look after itself, and it didn't happen again as far as I know.
But he got himself involved with attractive women all over
the place."

Rollison said, "Using your cottage and the flat as a
homing ground."

"Well, he always *had* used them," said Carruthers, "and
I didn't feel justified in saying that he had to stop. I mean,
I could more or less judge what was going on if I knew
where he was, couldn't I? I felt that I might be able to
help from time to time. And I'm not often in England, my
wife is a Parisienne and I prefer French cooking! Now
it's beginning to look as if he's really gone too far. What's
it all about, Rollison? Anything to do with this marriage?"

"Yes."

"Too bad about that, I know Barbara Lorne," said Carruthers. "She's a damned nice girl." He had never seemed
less like Holy Joe, but those beards *were* in the other
room.

"Of course it's never any use saying anything to a woman
in love, love's about the blindest thing I know when it
attacks a woman who's just realised that life can really be
something," Carruthers went on. "I did what I thought was
the best thing : I warned her father."

"*What?*"

Carruthers shrugged; and at last put his cigarette to his
lips and lit it.

"For the love of Pete, don't tell Guy I did that. But I had
to try to do something."

"When was this?"

"A year ago, I suppose."

"What did he say?"

"He told me that he'd stop the marriage somehow, and

I thought he was going to. I know that Guy wanted to get married nine months ago, but Barbara stalled, and I think that was out of consideration for her father. Then came the announcement of the wedding. I sent a gift, of course, and Guy wanted me to be present, but I couldn't bring myself. I mean, I can believe that some men will settle down after they've sown their wild oats, but how could I be sure of Guy? Certainly I couldn't do more than I had, could I?"

"No," agreed Rollison stonily.

"What *has* happened?" asked Carruthers.

Rollison explained, very simply, and watched the other's eyes. He saw the astonishment giving way to consternation, and then something that seemed very much like horror. Before he had finished, Carruthers was pacing the room, drawing and puffing at the cigarette. Was this acting?

"Helen *Good*man," he exclaimed. "Why, she was one of the nicest persons I've ever come across. Rollison, I can hardly believe it. I mean, she's just a country girl, pretty as a picture, so serene that there were times when she seemed almost simple. To take any kind of advantage of Helen— well, it's unthinkable. I knew she'd gone away and got married secretly, and she said her married name was Smith —but Guy! It's appalling." Carruthers broke off, and gulped. "He's always called himself Brown, down at the cottage. Did you know?"

"Yes," answered Rollison.

"As for this other woman—what's she like?" asked Carruthers.

Rollison described the dark-haired woman of the mews flat, and tried to imagine what Carruthers would look like in a beard.

"Can't say I can place her," said Carruthers. "She certainly isn't among my set. Haven't a photograph, have you?"

"No."

"Queer business," Carruthers said, and barked: "Queer

is hardly the word. It's a damned ugly business, too. Do you feel sure that Guy actually murdered these women?"

"A lot of people do," Rollison answered non-committally.

"He's going to be at a café round the corner—good God, he's due there any time, I'd forgotten! What the hell shall I do? I can't shelter him, can I? I mean, he might do a lot more harm if he's allowed to run around loose. It's a damned shame, if it hadn't been for that bloody wound, it would never have happened."

Rollison said, "Well, it's happened."

"What *shall* I do? Turn him over to the police?"

"I doubt if they could take any action yet, there aren't any extradition proceedings. Hasn't been time," went on Rollison. "Why do anything at all? Why not just tell him that you won't get mixed up in an affair like this, and that he can't come here."

"Will that help?"

"I would follow him."

"Ah, yes," said Carruthers. "That's your long suit, isn't it. Think you can make sure that he doesn't do any more harm?"

"Yes."

"Well, I don't mind admitting that I'd hate to feel that I'd sold him down the line," said Carruthers. "On the other hand, if I didn't know you were a pretty reliable customer in this kind of thing I'd have to do something. Er—think it might help if I were to talk? Lead him on, so to speak. I think he might—I say, Rollison! Supposing I bring him round here to have a chat, so that you can listen in? He would have no idea you were present, and I think I could make him talk where others can't."

"If he's a schizophrenic case, he can't talk because he won't know anything about the other side of his life."

"We can try," Carruthers urged, and his eyes were bright, as with a kind of hope. "I'll be back within a quarter of an hour."

"It might be a good idea, at that," agreed Rollison. He

thought of Lorne's chauffeur, in the cupboard where he himself would hide; there was grim irony about the suggestion. "How well do you know Bob Lorne?"

Carruthers grinned.

"Pretty well! He used to be a non-com in a regiment I was seconded to. You know how they've messed up the Army in recent years. I was seconded to a training establishment, must be twenty years ago, and Lorne was there. Believe it or not, he was as round in the belly then as he is now! He always had a genius for making money—he was the camp's unofficial bookmaker, I well remember. Interesting chap, always marvelled that he managed to produce something out of the bag like Barbara." He swung towards the door. "I'll go and fetch Guy, then. You'll treat him as gently as you can, won't you?"

"Yes," promised Rollison. "Do you know where Lorne stays when he's in Paris?"

"Oh, yes. He has an *appartement* in an old house near the Quai D'Orsay. It's a quiet retreat, sort of. The telephone's under the housekeeper's name, he only gives it to people whom he really wants to see. Why?"

"He's in Paris."

"Bob is? Good lord." Carruthers was fidgeting to get off. "Number 18, Rue Barbe, I forget the telephone number offhand. I've got it jotted down somewhere."

"Carruthers," said Rollison very quietly, "will you take a chance that I know what I'm doing?"

"Gladly."

"Don't bring Guy back here. Tell him where he can find Barbara and Lorne."

Carruthers said, "Are you crazy?"

"I have a queer idea that he's really in love with Barbara," said Rollison, "and I also have an idea that it would be a good thing to get him and Lorne face to face. How about it?"

Carruthers hesitated.

"Well, I suppose you know what you're doing. Sure Barbara's in Paris, too?"

"Yes."

"Right! Will you go along to Lorne's place?"

"I'll be there later," promised Rollison.

.   .   .   .   .

As soon as Carruthers had left the *appartement*, Rollison went to the cupboard, to find the chauffeur unconscious and badly in need of fresh air. Rollison sat him in a chair opposite a window, opened both window and shutter, and left him sitting there. He hurried out, half ran along the road towards the spot where he had told the taxi-driver to wait and found the shiny new Citroen there, the driver squatting on the window-sill of a shop opposite, reading a paper-backed book. He sprang to action when Rollison appeared, and his smile could not have been broader.

"Where to now, sir?"

"18, Rue Barbe. Do you know where that is?"

"Indeed I do," the cabby said. "It is near the Quai D'Orsay."

"That's it."

"Are you in a hurry?"

"I couldn't be in a greater one."

"*So*," breathed the driver.

Rollison sat back in his seat and watched the traffic falling behind them, and the traffic police watching the taxi almost with admiration. Soon they crossed the river, and the bridge beyond the one which led to the Ile de la Cité, and here the city seemed to be emptier. Only a few cars were parked, the tall, pale houses which overlooked the river had a deserted look; and a look of quality, also. The Rue Barbe was only fifty yards from the river, a small narrow turning with a few tall houses. Number 18 was almost at the corner. Rollison got out, and the cabby waited for his next orders.

"Just wait," Rollison said. "Watch this house in case I call you from a window."

"Very good, sir."

Rollison stepped from the taxi to tall brown varnished doors; and here again a small door was set in the large one; but he could not open this. He pressed a bell, and heard it ring inside. Soon a middle-aged concierge came out; a man with the look of an ex-prize-fighter.

"*M'sieu?*"

"I want to see Mr. Lorne, please."

"M. Lorne is not in, sir." His English was good.

Behind the man, in the wide cobbled yard, was a gleaming Chrysler, of red and black. There might be two cars of exactly the same make and colour scheme in Paris, but it wasn't likely. Rollison produced a thousand-franc note.

"This will find him in."

"Mr. Lorne is not in, sir."

Rollison said : "I'm sorry," and shot out his right hand and gripped the other's wrist, twisted, and sent him staggering back into the courtyard. He went in. A fountain of satyrs played in the centre, and even though the courtyard was surrounded on all four sides, the sun came through and turned it into liquid gold. The concierge had recovered, and looked as if he was preparing to counter-attack.

Rollison said, "Don't lie again. Tell Mr. Lorne I'm here."

The concierge looked up.

There was Lorne, leaning out of one of the windows, obviously attracted by the noise; as obviously he could see what had happened. Rollison had difficulty in bending his head back well enough to see him clearly.

"I will see no one !" Lorne called down in bad French.

"If you want to save your daughter's life you'll see me, now," Rollison said, and his words travelled clear and sharp. "Tell this man to let me up."

There was a moment of hesitation; and then Lorne said as if helplessly :

"Oh, all right." He dropped into that execrable French again, and the concierge reluctantly went to a glass door which led to the hall and to a flight of wide stairs; a staircase which could not have been more handsome. The walls were padded and the handrail shone. The concierge stood at the foot of the steps, and Rollison glanced down from the first floor, then went up to the second.

Lorne opened the door.

"What's all this about my daughter?" he demanded roughly.

"I'll ask the questions," Rollison said, and thrust the little ball of a man inside, closed the door and shot the bolt. "Two, for a start. Why did you try to have me stopped in London, and why did you tell the Chrysler chauffeur to put me out of action?"

"Because I don't trust you," Lorne said viciously. "I've been warned about you."

21

LAP OF LUXURY

THEY stood in a square hall. Electric light from two chandeliers made it seem pleasantly bright. The walls were panelled in satin, and the furniture looked as if it had been preserved in perfect condition for hundreds of years. The carpet looked to be of hand-made tapestry. Everything was luxurious, but there was no ostentation; no bad taste.

The little ball that was Robert Lorne stood in the middle of the hall, glaring at Rollison; there was something pathetic about him.

"Who warned you?" Rollison demanded.

"That doesn't matter."

"What did they say?"

"They told me what I ought to have known for myself, all you're interested in is what you can get out of this. You might as well save your breath, Rollison, I've nothing to say to you."

"What did they tell you?" Rollison insisted. "That if I discovered the truth I'd blackmail you even worse than they're doing?"

Lorne caught his breath.

"Is that it?" Rollison demanded, and went nearer; he hardly needed telling that it was true, the way Lorne had collapsed was virtual proof of what he had suspected. "All right," Rollison went on roughly, "we'll see how it works out, because I'm going to find out just what's behind these killings. Where's your daughter?"

"She's resting."

"Has she come round from the injection?"

Lorne said, "Who—who told you——?"

"Your chauffeur told me," Rollison said. "He thought it was safe, he didn't think I'd get away. Where is Barbara?"

"It's no use, she'll be unconscious for another three or four hours," Lorne answered. "I had to do it, I had to get this dreadful business finished before she came round again."

"What dreadful business?"

"Why don't you use your head?" Lorne almost screeched. "I've got to make her understand that she can't go on with Lessing. She's got to understand."

"And how are you proposing to stop her?"

Lorne gulped. "I—I'll be able to do it, once he's here."

"Now how did you guess that he was coming here?" asked Rollison softly.

"He knew where my Paris *appartement* is, he was bound to come here sooner or later."

"It could be," conceded Rollison. "Where's Barbara?" When Lorne did not answer, he moved towards tall double doors in one corner. "And where are the servants? All sent out, so that you can finish this little game your own way?"

"Rollison, don't try to wake Barbara up."

"First, I'll make sure that she's asleep," Rollison said, and pushed open the double doors. They led into a luxurious room, much larger than the hall, a beautiful *salon* with a grand piano lost in it; there was room for forty people here, in comfort. Other doors led off, on two sides, and Rollison went towards the right, knowing that if he went left it would be towards the windows overlooking the courtyard. Lorne followed him. Lorne could not be trusted, but at the moment he was nervous, not sure what would happen if Rollison turned on him.

There was a passage, and three doors.

In the first room, next to the *salon*, Barbara lay, sleeping or unconscious.

Rollison went inside.

She looked quite lovely, although she was deathly pale.

Her eyes were closed, and Rollison had not realised how sweeping her lashes were, nor how glossy black they looked against her skin. She seemed to be breathing evenly. He took her hands and felt for the pulse; it was a little slow. Judging from what he could see, her father was right : she would not come round for several hours.

He turned to Lorne.

"What makes you think you can lead her life for her?"

"She's infatuated by this devil, who——"

"She is married to Guy Lessing."

"She isn't, it was only a form of marriage !"

"He was not married to anyone else previously," said Rollison.

"But you saw that certificate ! You know about the second Mrs. Lessing."

"Oh, I know about the Mrs. Lessings," Rollison said, "and I know that they were murdered. But not by Guy."

Lorne gasped. "They were murdered by Lessing, and I'm going to make sure that he can't do my daughter any harm." Lorne snatched his hand out of his pocket, and Rollison saw the gun in it. "Understand? I'm going to shoot him dead when he comes in. I'll make sure that he can't do any harm."

Lorne was gasping for breath.

And then a man spoke from behind Rollison :

"You're not going to stop him, either," he said. "Raise your hands, and don't move."

.   .   .   .

It was Holy Joe.

And it was Carruthers, betrayed by his clear blue eyes. He had changed his clothes, his hair was dark brown instead of fair and his wig was almost as natural-looking as a real one; but it was Guy's friend, Carruthers.

He must have come swiftly ahead of Rollison.

.   .   .   .   .

Holy Joe held an automatic pistol in his large hand. While Lorne kept Rollison covered, Holy Joe Carruthers ran his hands over him, found the gas pistol and confiscated it, then found the automatic and dropped it into his own pocket.

He said very thoughtfully, "You'd have a British licence for that gun, wouldn't you?" He was holding it by the muzzle, gingerly. "And it would have your fingerprints on, wouldn't it?"

"What nice thought is this, Carruthers?' asked Rollison quietly.

"Spotted me as quickly as that, have you?" Carruthers said, grinning; that made his identity even more obvious. "Well, that doesn't matter—no one saw me come in—as Carruthers—they only saw a bearded man. And I'm sure you wouldn't give me away, would you?"

"Just as soon as I get the chance," Rollison said. "So you killed Helen, and you nipped round the back way and killed your wife . . ."

"Lady-friend," said Carruthers softly. "You know too much and you guess too much, but you're going to be a great help." He pulled off the beard sharply; it was quite astonishing that it had looked so real. He tossed it aside, and went on :

"Wouldn't it be a remarkable thing if you discovered your old friend Guy Lessing was a scoundrel, after all, and that in order to stop him from getting away you shot him. A pretty touch indeed. Don't you think so, Bob?"

Lorne said, "It—it would be brilliant." There was a moment of hesitation, but Carruthers did not seem to notice that.

"As an outraged parent you would have all the sympathy of a French jury," went on Carruthers, "and of nearly all the newspaper readers, too. France is such a civilised country, there's none of the puritan sternness which makes England so unbearable. But it would be much better if you didn't have to stand trial, wouldn't it? After all, Barbara won't mind if Rollison shoots—in fact, Bob, we're going to find it much better this way." He laughed. "It was a mistake to be frightened of Rollison, I should never have told you to try to shake him off."

Rollison was standing very still; calculating.

"Who will care if Barbara hates the sight of Rollison and the very sound of his name?" asked Carruthers. "It would be much better to let her think he'd killed Guy than to make her hate you for the rest of your life. Why, there'll be a touching reconciliation. Don't you think so, Rollison?"

"What am I to be?" asked Rollison. "Dumb?"

"You couldn't be dumber than you are," said Carruthers, and he sounded too gay for that to be a sneer. "Think of the evidence. Your fingerprints on your gun. Bob Lorne's testimony, because he saw you do it. Didn't he, Bob?"

Lorne didn't speak.

"I don't think you'd be able to talk yourself out of that one," said Carruthers, with a grin which still looked pleasant and friendly. "I've sent the servants away, too—no one else will know what's happened. So we'll be rid of poor old Guy, and he won't have any more worries about his mental health. You'll be in bad with the French, and lucky if you don't see the inside of a French prison; they're not at all comfortable, I'm told. You can name me, but I've a beautiful alibi—I've not been out of England this week. My passport's stamped—I used another one for Holy Joe Smith!"

"Helen Goodman Smith," Rollison said heavily.

"So clever," sneered Carruthers. "Well, it's worked out fine. I was actually hoping that we would be able to finish the job in Paris. So much more convenient."

"What job in particular?" asked Rollison, still mildly.

"And you haven't got as far as that," Carruthers jeered. "You were wrong, Bob, he's not so clever—he hasn't guessed."

Lorne said in a strangled voice, "Don't take too much for granted, he's smarter than you think."

"He used to be smart, but he's getting past it," said Carruthers. But he looked very thoughtful; no one could possibly have clearer blue eyes, and no one could look more honest than he. "I'm just wondering if we could make a clean break with both of them. Two die in a duel, so to speak. Or whether——" He broke off, as if he was considering that very deeply. "Don't slacken your grip on your gun, Bob, he looks as if he might jump at you."

Lorne didn't speak, but stepped back a yard.

"I'll tell you one thing," Carruthers announced abruptly. "Rollison may be getting long in the tooth, but he still has a kind of gallantry complex. Haven't you, Toff? He'll probably call out to warn Guy, so we'd better make sure that he can't."

He moved, behind Rollison; and the gun in Lorne's pale, plump hand was very steady.

"Quite sure that Guy will come?" asked Rollison.

"Oh, he'll come. I had time to nip round and have a word with him. I told him that Barbara was here, and wanted to see him. He's due at six o'clock, and I'll be surprised if he isn't here dead on the dot, so that gives him about ten minutes. He'll be roaring for Barbara, longing to explain how he's been maligned and maltreated; Barbara will be about the last thing he will roar for."

He was doing something behind Rollison's back; there was a rustling sound. He might have a scarf, a handkerchief, sticking-plaster; certainly it would be something with which he could gag Rollison. If there was a chance, it was here and now.

They had an automatic apiece, and Rollison's lay on the table, in front of his eyes. Could he call that a chance? He had come, believing that Guy Lessing would walk into a trap, but also believing that he could spring it before it closed on Guy. He couldn't now. He did not know much about Carruthers, and was not sure of the association between him and Lorne, but he was quite sure that Carruthers was deadly behind that friendly smile.

"Bob," he said to Lorne, "if you let this happen, you'll have this murder and two others on your conscience. You know that Lessing didn't kill those women, and you know that he wasn't married to them, don't you?"

Lorne just stared at him, gun steady in his hand.

"That will be quite something to live with," Rollison went on.

"Oh, Bob won't mind," declared Carruthers, and it was easy to believe that his breath was warm on the back of Rollison's neck. "He's had something to live with for a long time. Haven't you, Bob? We've come to terms now."

"Bob," insisted Rollison, "you shouldn't let him get away with it. What has he got against you to blackmail you like this? You're becoming an accessory to murder. Don't you understand that? They would never get you for the others, but if you let this happen——"

Carruthers tapped him, quite lightly, on the swollen bruise on the nape of his neck; a rabbit punch which was almost gentle, yet which sent pain streaking through Rollison.

He winced.

"Painful?" asked Carruthers, as if with concern. "Well, I must say that it looks as if it could be a lot better. Stop trying to bait our Bob. No one is going to get him or me for the death of Major Guy Lessing. You'll be one witness against two, if you live to be questioned. Any bright ideas, Bob?"

Rollison felt a swift movement behind him, and then something appeared in front of his eyes. He saw a handkerchief stretched tight between Carruthers' two hands, and before he could avoid it, it was pulled against his mouth, forcing his lips back, forcing his head back, bringing agony to the back of his neck. Swiftly, Carruthers tied a knot; and tied it again while Rollison tried to twist round, but Lorne kept him covered.

Carruthers let him go, and laughed.

"That's about it," he said. "Guy should be here in five

minutes. Don't stand up, Rollison, you've had a tiring day. Take a chair." He took Rollison's arm and lowered him into a chair. Then he moved away, and squatted on the corner of a beautifully polished table, nursing the gun in his right hand, watching Rollison and the door at the same time.

Lessing wouldn't be long, now.

22

ARRIVAL

THERE was the sound of a car outside, the first to pass along here for several minutes. Carruthers went to the window and looked out; the shutters were open a crack. He seemed anxious, but suddenly relaxed and smiled. He turned towards Lorne, and said :

"He's here, walking right into it."

Lorne made no answer.

Carruthers said, "Don't let anything Rollison said make you go back on what we've arranged, Bob. Life wouldn't be very good for you if you did. Go and sit on the other side of the room."

Slowly, Lorne obeyed.

The car stopped outside, and almost at once a door slammed; someone was in a hurry. Footsteps came, quick and light; then there was a long pause. No doubt Lessing was pressing the bell, and the concierge was going to open the door now. He would allow Lessing to come right up.

Carruthers still had his own gun in his right hand. He went to the table and picked up Rollison's, and Rollison saw that he had pulled on a cotton glove, the kind a Frenchman was likely to wear when travelling by train. He had come prepared for everything. He was still smiling, and it was easy to believe that he would smile as Lessing came in, and as he fired.

If he fired.

"Watch Rollison, Bob," he said.

A buzzer sounded, obviously the front-door bell of the flat itself. Neither of the men moved. Carruthers weighed both guns, as if measuring one against the other, and there was tension in his smile. Voices sounded, so one servant was still here. Then footsteps came, and the door began to open.

Rollison leapt to his feet.

He swung round, grabbed the back of the chair and swung it. He saw Lorne glaring at him, saw the gun raised, and flung the chair at Carruthers and at the door. He heard the sharp sound of the shot from Lorne's gun; then something hit him in the left shoulder, and spun him round. The effort had been so great that he was already off his balance, and now went staggering; he could not see what happened at the door. He caught a glimpse of Lessing; Lessing must see what was happening, must be able to guess at the deadly danger.

There was a second shot.

The door slammed, and Rollison believed that Lessing had seen the danger and slammed the door before the bullet reached him. Carruthers was leaping at the door, one gun tossed aside, his free hand thrust towards the handle of the door.

Rollison was going for the gun, which had landed on a chair. Lorne had fired once and hurt him badly enough; he would probably fire again, and now only two yards separated them, if Lorne shot to kill he could hardly miss.

Carruthers had the door wide open.

Lorne fired again.

This bullet struck the seat of the chair on which the other gun lay, and sent it rocketing forward. It toppled over the edge, and clattered to the floor. Carruthers was outside, and his and Lessing's footsteps were thudding. Lorne was standing with the gun in his hand, and making himself say:

"Keep back, Rollison, or I'll kill you. Keep back."

Rollison could not utter a word.

There was the gun almost within hand's reach; he needed only a second to get it. Carruthers offered no immediate danger. But there was a glint as of madness in Lorne's eyes, here was a man driven to the absolute limit of desperation;

the gun which had once been steady was quivering in his hand.

Rollison went for the chair, grabbed it with his right hand and slid it along the floor towards the fat man. Lorne skipped to one side. Rollison dived for the gun, and heard another shot; but this one missed. He had the gun in his hand and swung round, shooting at Lorne. He knew that the fat man was trying to screw up his courage to shoot again, but he could not; and Rollison's bullet caught him in the chest. He went backwards, little legs working like pistons, hit against a chair and sprawled down. Rollison saw his gun fall. He went as swiftly as he could, but his left arm was numb, he felt as if he had no shoulder.

For as long as Lorne remained conscious, he was a threat. Rollison turned the gun in his hand and struck the man on the temple, hard enough to knock him out, then turned round with the gun the right way round. The footsteps had stopped. He heard a man speak, but could not distinguish the words. He slipped the gun into his pocket and pulled at the knot in the handkerchief at the back of his neck, but it was tied too tightly for him to release it with one hand.

He heard a door slam, *behind him*.

That was the door leading to the bedroom where the girl lay sleeping.

He heard bolts shot home.

Then Carruthers said, quite clearly if a little breathlessly :

"You'd better think again, Guy, if you want to see your wife alive again. She's here, with me."

.   .   .   .   .   .

Rollison stood there, unable to speak a word, knowing that the wound was bleeding freely, that he could not hope to keep on his feet much longer. He heard the threat, and believed that Carruthers would carry it out. He did not hear Lessing, and he could not call Lessing. He plucked savagely at the knot, but instead of loosening it, seemed to make it tighter.

Then this door opened cautiously, and Guy Lessing came in.

.   .   .   .   .

The almost unbelievable thing was that he looked quite calm and self-possessed, and as immaculate as ever. If he had hurried, he showed no sign of it. He saw Rollison, showed momentary surprise, and then looked at Lorne; it was impossible to guess what he was thinking about Lorne, except to be sure that he had no liking for the man.

He spoke quietly.

"You all right?" Then he shifted his gaze and saw Rollison's shoulder, and blood trickling down the back of Rollison's left hand. "Like that, is it?" he said, and came across, taking a penknife from his pocket. "Turn round." He began to cut the handkerchief, and Rollison was almost beyond feeling the pain at the back of his neck.

The gag fell apart.

"Can you talk?" asked Lessing, still very quietly.

Rollison's lips were already stiff, but he had not been gagged long enough to make him speechless.

"Barbara's in that room."

Lessing's eyes narrowed. "Positive?"

"I saw her twenty minutes ago."

Lessing said, "The hell you did." He stared at the door as he went on, "There's another door, through the kitchen, but that's locked and bolted, too, and he'll have made sure we can't get in."

"Guy," called Carruthers from the next room, quite clearly and calmly, "I mean exactly what I say."

Lessing answered in exactly the same even tone of voice, and nothing in his expression suggested anger. But there was a bite in the words.

"I'm sure you do, you've had a lot of practice. Exactly what do you want?"

"I want you and Rollison to leave by the front door, and then cross the river. I can see you on the other side. Just do that, that's all."

"What about Barbara?"

"Barbara will be all right," said Carruthers. The most remarkable thing about all this was the conversational tone of each man. "She won't have so much money as you once thought, but love will make up for that, won't it?"

"What will happen to her money?"

"You wouldn't put filthy lucre above the life of your bride, would you?"

"I don't know," answered Lessing. "I've known you for so long that I may have caught the complaint."

"Don't try to be funny, Guy."

"You can take it from me that I'm not trying to be funny," said Lessing. "What will happen to her money?"

"At the moment she controls a lot more than she needs," Carruthers said. "Lorne gave her a fortune, and so did her mother. She'll make over most of this to her father, and he will make me a free gift of most of it. There are one or two little indiscretions in his past that he's anxious to pay for."

"Ah," said Lessing, and then turned to Rollison and went on : "He has Barbara, we have Lorne. Is it worth the gamble of taking Lorne with us?"

Carruthers started to speak, but didn't finish.

"Or would it be better to kill Lorne now?" asked Lessing, and his voice was still quite conversational. "If he's dead, he can't take over Barbara's money, and I doubt whether Carruthers' claim would stand up in a court of law. And if he's dead, Barbara won't have to go through all the agony of explanation and probably the trial. What do you think?"

Carruthers called, sharply, "You'd better think clearly. You get out, and leave Lorne where he is."

"With Lorne dead your future certainly wouldn't be so rosy," said Lessing. "Ralph."

"Just get out."

"Carruthers, listen," Rollison interrupted. "Lessing has something there. Remember your own idea? To let me kill him, so that you and Lorne could get away with everything? Remember being so glad that Barbara was unconscious and couldn't hear a thing?"

"You leave this to Lessing," Carruthers answered; but now his voice betrayed an increasing tension. "Guy, get out."

"Pretty thought, wasn't it?" Lessing said, and he was actually grinning at Rollison. "You see what I mean when I say that being close to you for so long might make crime contagious. Barbara will never know who killed her father, and she certainly won't believe you."

"She'll believe me," said Carruthers, and there was a moment's pause, as if he were getting breathless. "And even if she didn't, she'd have doubts about it. Every time she looked at you, she would wonder whether you had killed her poor old dad. Don't let Rollison fool you. Get out, and take him with you. It's the only way you'll save Barbara's life."

·　　　·　　　·　　　·　　　　　·

Lessing turned to Rollison, and mouthed one sentence.
"He means it."

Rollison said, "He knows that it's the only way he can win, and if he's going to lose, he'll probably kill her. He's got two murders to his credit already."

"Can you prove that?"

"I think I can give the police what they need, now. His only hope is to keep a tight hold on Barbara or her father— tight enough to keep us quiet." Rollison went closer to Lessing, and whispered very softly, "I'll keep him talking. You try the window."

Lessing did not speak, but simply turned away. The shutters were pulled to but were not locked, and he opened them wider, then stepped on to the tiny balcony.

·　　　·　　　·　　　·　　　　　·　·

A dozen times, perhaps twice as often, Rollison had taken desperate chances in a life which had been starred with risk. He dared not take one now. His left arm hung limp, and the wound in the shoulder was beginning to throb; he would not have had a chance outside. But it was worse, standing here, and knowing that another man was taking that chance.

He was staring at the window and the tiny balcony beyond.

He had studied these from the outside, and knew that several feet separated one balcony from another; that it would be taking one's life in one's hand to jump. Lessing would attempt it; Lessing had all the qualities of courage and of heroism that it needed; but could he possibly succeed?

Rollison would have given a fortune to have the chance, to take the risk that Lessing was taking now.

Carruthers called, "What are you two talking about?"

Rollison whispered, just loudly enough for the sound to reach Lessing; then whispered again, as if Lessing were answering back.

"Don't try any tricks!" Carruthers called sharply, "I've got the shutters open, I can see the window from here. And if he kills Lorne, I'll kill Barbara!"

"Don't you think I know?" Rollison said, as if in anguish, and then raised his voice sharply, speaking as if Lessing were still in the room; Rollison could not see him, but could just see his shadow, and knew that he was poised on the iron balcony. He seemed to be swaying.

"*Keep away from Lorne!*" Rollison shouted.

"Guy, don't be a fool, I mean what I say." Carruthers was trying not to screech, but could not conceal his desperation; a live Lorne was vital to him.

"Lorne, look out!" Rollison shouted, and with his right hand gripped the back of a chair and sent it crashing down, thumped the floor with his foot, staggered against the table and made it rock; and he actually let himself fall, so that

Carruthers could have no doubt that someone had fallen. The fall jolted him painfully, but he spoke as if he were gasping for breath.

"All right, Carruthers, now let's talk terms. Lorne means nothing to me, you can do what you like with him. But if you don't hand his daughter over, you'll never get Lorne alive. What's it to be?"

That was when he saw Lorne open his eyes.

But Lorne was not important in that moment, only Lessing mattered. Had he made that jump? There had been no thud from the courtyard, but the noise of climbing could have been drowned.

Rollison backed to the window, and to the balcony, acutely aware that Lorne was watching him.

He glanced across.

Lessing was hanging by his arms from the other balcony. He had made the jump and nearly missed, and now he could not climb up. He dared not drop the sixty feet to the cobbles, for that would break his bones, and almost certainly kill him.

He was clinging by his fingers, and would not be able to stay like that for long; he had to be helped up, or else he would crash down.

Carruthers called, "I won't make a deal until you and Lessing are on the other side of the river. I won't hurt the girl, you'll have to take my word for it."

As he spoke, Lorne was getting to his feet.

And Lessing hung there, eyes turned towards Rollison as he twisted round and looked over his shoulder.

He called in a whispering voice :

"Don't worry about me. Save Barbara."

23

SAVE BARBARA

ROLLISON heard the words clearly, and Lorne must have heard them, too. He was on one knee. Rollison saw that, but Lorne seemed hardly to matter. He was helpless, even without the danger from Carruthers; he could not act at all to save Guy Lessing. Here was failure; utter, desolating failure. He could not see how it could end, could not see any hope. The girl helpless, Lessing likely to fall and smash himself to pieces, he himself so weak from pain and loss of blood that he could hardly stand.

The nearness of complete disaster made him feel even worse; and his legs were weak.

Then he saw the gun in Lorne's hand.

He should have known about that; should have realised that Lorne had fallen near the table; and when he had knocked against the table to make Carruthers think that he and Lessing were fighting the gun had fallen.

Now Lorne had it.

There was a cut on the man's lips, and a puffy swelling on one of the fat, round cheeks. One of his eyes was closing, too, yet he looked oddly immaculate as he stood to his full height. There was a kind of dignity about him; he was more the Lorne of the wedding breakfast than the Lorne of to-day.

"I'll give you five minutes to get Lessing away," Carruthers called. "If I don't see you crossing the street by then——"

"It's all right," Lorne called, in an unsteady voice. "It's all right, I've got him covered."

"*Bob!*"

"I've got Rollison covered," insisted Lorne, and then he raised his voice; for a despairing moment Rollison thought that the end had come, for Lorne raised the gun and fired.

But he fired a yard wide of Rollison.

"What's that?" Carruthers cried.

"It's all right," Lorne called again, "you won't have anything else to worry about with Rollison, he's finished. And Lessing's unconscious."

He was standing and covering the door.

"Come on," he called. "I'm in a hell of a mess."

There was a thud of footsteps, the handle of the door turned and then Carruthers came striding in. He was grinning broadly, and looked on top of the world. In that moment he must have been quite sure that he had triumphed, had thrust all thought of failure behind him.

He looked big and handsome and likeable—until he saw Lorne.

He stopped in his tracks.

"What the devil——?" he began, but couldn't go on.

Rollison held his own gun now, steady in his right hand, and Carruthers would never know how near he was to collapsing, or guess what an effort it was to keep the gun level.

"From the beginning I told you not to let Barbara suffer," Lorne said, in a tense voice. "And you always told me that the only danger to Barbara came from Lessing. Well, I know better now. He's just risked his life to save her, and you—well, I heard every word you said. Now I'm going to kill you, Carruthers, because of all the things you've done to me, and the harm you would do to Barbara."

Carruthers gasped. "Bob, don't be crazy! I was only bluffing, I wouldn't have hurt her."

"You wouldn't?" echoed Lorne. "Well, let's see if this will hurt you."

Carruthers realised that the fat man meant to shoot, and leapt at him; and as he leapt, Lorne fired. Carruthers seemed to stop in mid-air. There was a look of bewilderment on his face, as if he had not believed that this could happen.

He crumpled up, with a bullet in his chest.

Rollison ejaculated, "*Watch him!*" and made himself hurry into the passage. He went into the bedroom, where Barbara lay unconscious. He felt as if his left arm would fall off, and at moments his legs threatened to collapse under him, but he reached the balcony. He saw Lessing's fingers, still gripping; but slipping. He went down on one knee, and put his right hand through the railings of the balcony, and gripped Lessing's wrist.

He said, "I'll pull, you try and get a grip on a railing."

There was sweat on Lessing's face, and Rollison knew that the man could not hold on more than a few seconds longer; and he wondered whether he could find the strength to give him a chance to get up. He set his teeth, and pulled. He felt Lessing's weight, like a ton on his right arm and shoulder. He gritted his teeth and held on. With agonising slowness Lessing's hand and wrist came through the railings; then Lessing seemed to swing his right arm, and grip the iron.

"Can't hold on long," Rollison gasped. "Heave."

"I'll be all right, now." Lessing released Rollison's hand, and grabbed a railing with his own free hand; now it was easy. He hauled himself up until he got a foot on the edge of the balcony. Rollison was leaning against the shutters of the window, and he could just see Lessing, as through a kind of mist.

"Thank Lorne," he managed to say. "Lorne shot Carruthers. Thank Lorne."

"Good God!" Lessing exclaimed. "Miracles."

.   .   .   .   .

Rollison was in the ward of a hospital or nursing home; he didn't know which, for he had been unconscious when he had come here. His left shoulder was heavily bandaged, but he felt free from pain. He was going over much that had happened in a lazy kind of way. He hardly deserved a trophy from this case, although he need not blame himself too much, for he had been made almost *hors de combat* from very early on, and had never properly recovered. On the credit side, too, was the fact that he had not been fooled for long by Carruthers' manner, and had been quick to see the importance of Holy Joe.

He'd talked a way into gaining time, too, so that Lorne . . .

He wondered where and how Lorne was; and Barbara; and Lessing.

Had he been here for an hour or two or a day or two? Until he could check with a nurse, he could only guess; operations often took a long time and recovery from the anæsthetic longer. But he was so comfortable, with dope of course, that he hardly cared whether he had been here for hours or days. He could even smile a little at the thought of the moment when Barbara had appeared at his flat; the runaway bride who need not have run away.

"One of these days I'd like to know all about it," Rollison said aloud, then closed his eyes and drifted off to sleep.

. . . . .

He sat up in bed, not quite sure how much later it was, but in a very different mood. He was fully alert. The haziness had gone, and Lessing was sitting by the side of the bed, very handsome, still rather tight-lipped although smiling.

"How's Barbara?" Rollison inquired.

"Very well, thanks, and sends her love."

"Give her mine," said Rollison, and realised that there was no tension at all in Lessing. "How about Lorne?"

'You might say that there has been a complete reconciliation," Lessing declared. "I doubt whether he and I will ever actually *like* each other, but we have acquired what you might call mutual respect."

"I can imagine that," said Rollison. "What was the business all about?"

"That's a tall order," Lessing said, and smiled a little more freely. "From the beginning, or——"

"Who married those women in your name? Was it Carruthers?"

"It was just after I'd had the head injury, and was convalescent. I had some lapses of memory and black-outs. I made a joke of it. So did Carruthers. He was already married, but wanted company in London as well as Paris. Helen Goodman was a simple soul, and 'marriage' was the easy way to get her. She'd never known me as Lessing, only Brown. Carruthers married her as Guy Lessing, and persuaded her to keep it secret, saying his family objected. By Helen's standards he kept her well supplied with money, and promised that he'd win his family round. He used my name because he couldn't use his own; it was as simple as that, to begin with."

Lessing paused, and made Rollison realise how anxious he was to hear the rest.

"What I didn't suspect was that the man I'd known and trusted all my life was utterly corrupt," Lessing went on. "The use of my name was almost incidental. At that time he was already blackmailing Robert Lorne. In his early days, before he made a lot of money, Lorne wasn't particularly scrupulous. Barbara doesn't know, and I hope she need never find out, but he defrauded a lot of people. He first began to make money by buying surplus army stores, using a small business that he owned outside the Army, and he was also among the men who valued the surplus goods. Carruthers was the officer in charge of some of this disposal; he discovered what had happened, and cut himself in. They worked together for years. But Lorne used his money to make a fortune in industry and commerce, and Carruthers gambled and lived fast. Finally, Lorne refused to pay him more money. What Lorne didn't know was that Carruthers had kept a close watch on him, and knew about one or two other frauds. The two were deadlocked when Lorne's wife died, and left her fortune to Barbara. Lorne also made a large part of his money over to Barbara, to avoid death duties, and so keep it out of Carruthers' reach. Carruthers had no hold over Barbara, and couldn't be sure how she would react if he blackmailed her by threatening to disclose her father's past crimes——"

"All old crimes?" interrupted Rollison.

"Yes, and mostly to do with tax frauds," Lessing answered. "Lorne felt he was on top, until Barbara and I decided to get married. Carruthers had introduced us, and Lorne thought that I was hand-in-glove with him. No doubt you remember Lorne's opposition," Lessing added dryly.

"I remember."

"I never understood why he was so bitterly opposed," went on Lessing. "He's told me now that he accused Carruthers of trying to control Barbara through me—and apparently that caught Carruthers on the raw, and made Lorne realise that he was wrong. Of course, Carruthers saw me marrying the fortune he'd been working to get for years." Lessing smiled twistedly. "That was too much, and yet he knew that he had no hope of marrying Barbara; his money would come direct from Lorne if it came from anyone.

"He needed to get control of Lorne again, break down Lorne's resistance and make Barbara sign over her fortune to her father. He had the old bigamous marriage in my name as a possible weapon, and also had his identity as Holy Joe to help him. He'd blackmailed a lot of people for years—getting knowledge of the skeletons in their cupboards as Carruthers, and extorting blackmail through contacts who knew him only as Holy Joe."

Lessing paused, but Rollison did not prompt him.

"That was the situation, then," Lessing went on, speaking more sharply. "Neither Ellerby or I can see exactly how Carruthers' mind worked afterwards. My wedding was drawing near, but stopping the marriage wouldn't help Carruthers, for the strength of his position as a blackmailer lay in holding threat of disclosure of my 'marriage' to Helen Goodman over my head and Lorne's. I'd be in no position to deny it if Helen was dead and couldn't identify her husband. Carruthers obviously wanted Barbara and me to marry. So why should he tell Barbara about the other 'marriage' and send that certificate?"

"My dear chap!" protested Rollison.

"Now what?"

"Is Ellerby puzzled by this, too?"

"He says so." Lessing's manner became challenging. "Aren't you?"

'Not now that it's so obvious that Carruthers couldn't cash-in until the marriage," Rollison said. "Did Ellerby talk freely?"

"Very."

"Did he say if anyone picked up a packet of £100 at any of the calling addresses?"

"No one did."

"That always stank to high heaven," Rollison said. "There were no fingerprints on the envelopes or certificates that Barbara or Lorne received, but the obvious assumption was that the same person sent each. The obvious is too often wrong. Ask Ellerby! The story told us was false, of course, probably put up by Carruthers to mislead the police or me. It explained why Lorne was so worried yet hid the real truth—that Carruthers was getting his claws into him again."

Lessing began to smile.

"Quite right," he confirmed. "Lorne's told me that."

"But not Ellerby?"

"No, and no one will tell the police if I can stop it. Rolly, who else would want to warn Barbara not to marry me?"

"False premise," Rollison replied promptly. "There was no one 'else', and Carruthers undoubtedly wanted the marriage. One person didn't want it, though."

"Who?"

"The woman who thought she was Mrs. Guy Lessing," Rollison answered gently, and Lessing drew in a sharp breath.

"Helen?"

"Helen Goodman, who undoubtedly read about the forthcoming wedding," agreed Rollison. "What was more reasonable than that she should make a desperate attempt to stop the wedding? She wouldn't know what to do when she failed, lacking the courage to get inside the church and call out. We can be sure that Carruthers—probably as Holy Joe—persuaded her to go back to Rufus Cottage. I've little doubt that his shouting was to distract Helen as much as alarm Lorne on the church steps. There's no doubt that Carruthers was at the cottage when I arrived, and killed Helen. That's a relief of a kind," Rollison went on quietly. "He would have killed her to keep her quiet, because she could have cleared you. She wasn't killed because I went there. His own wife could betray him, too. I've no doubt that he told her to tell me that she was Mrs. Lessing; knowing he was within earshot, she was too frightened not to. But she wouldn't be able to stand much questioning from the police or from me, so he had to kill her."

"He had accomplices, of course——"

"The chauffeur from Paris was one; we know he was in England at the time of the murders," Lessing interrupted. "He went back to Paris on an aircraft ahead of you. And Carruthers used several men from time to time, and sent them to try to keep you from going to Paris. He'd had Barbara watched, and she led to you."

Rollison considered all this for a moment or two, and then asked:

"What about the part Lorne played at the end?"

Lessing shrugged.

"He says that he was prepared to do whatever Carruthers ordered in order to save Barbara, and there's no doubt Lorne realised that Carruthers, if he'd lost out, would have disclosed everything discreditable in Lorne's past," Lessing said at last. "He made amends, whatever his motives."

"He made the fullest possible amends," Rollison agreed soberly. He sat silent, feeling unexpectedly tired, and almost solemn while he contemplated how near death he had been, and how much he owed to Lorne.

Lessing stood up suddenly.

"I've overstayed the time I was allowed, as you're still an invalid," he said. "How do you feel, Rolly?"

"Nearly fighting fit."

"I'd like to see you when you're really fighting fit," said Lessing, and smiled warmly as he pressed Rollison's arm. "I want just to say thanks," he added, and went out.

. . . . .

Three weeks later, Rollison stepped unaided off the aircraft at the London airport, and by a special dispensation, Jolly came forward before he reached Customs. Jolly looked brown and fit, and his eyes were glowing.

"You ought to have a month without me every year, it would make a new man of you," greeted Rollison. "It's good to be back."

"And very good to have you back, sir," Jolly said. He saw Rollison through all the formalities, as if Rollison needed protecting, led the way to the Rolls-Bentley and helped Rollison in, and took the wheel himself. "I think Major Lessing gave you most of the details, sir," he went on, "and I expect you know that he and Mrs. Lessing are now in Cornwall, finishing their honeymoon. Mr. Lorne has been released on bail after being charged with certain frauds, and several of Major Carruthers' associates are in custody, awaiting trial; Major Carruthers himself is likely to be well enough to appear at the magistrate's court next week. However, the end of the case might now be called a foregone conclusion."

"Fine," approved Rollison. "Did you see Mrs. Lessing before she left?"

"She called to leave a message for you," said Jolly, and said no more about that until they were in the big room, and Rollison was looking at the trophy wall, his head on the side, his eyes holding a new light.

For draped in a position specially made for it by Jolly, was Barbara Lessing's bridal veil.

"There is her message, sir," said Jolly.

THE END

ALSO BY JOHN CREASEY

A SIX FOR THE TOFF

The Toff had been looking forward to playing spectator—at a cricket match, not a murder

The call for help from an American jewel collector had been no more than an annoyance to the Hon. Richard Rollison. But the girl who led him to one man run down by a killer-car, and to another with a knife in his throat, made him take the call far more seriously.

When the American disappears, the Toff is left chasing a very cold trail; and when every lead ends in murder, it is clear that he, too, is batting on a dangerously sticky wicket.

World wide sales of John Creasey's books total over 65,000,000 copies.
THE TOFF
is his most engaging character.

IN CORONET BOOKS

ALSO BY JOHN CREASEY

DOUBLE FOR THE TOFF

The Toff certainly didn't want to take on two problems at once, but these were entreaties he couldn't ignore

He was needed by Robert Benning—accused of murdering the beautiful and promiscuous Marjorie Fryer—and his mother and girlfriend, both desolate and desperate for help.

He was needed by young Cedric Dwight—with his so-called delusions and his genuine fears, especially when he was taken away by men, who might not kill, but certainly aimed to terrify him.

And then quite suddenly, there was Bill Ebbutt— owner of an East End boxing gymnasium and a staunch friend of the Toff—to avenge as well.

World wide sales of John Creasey's books total over 65,000,000 copies.
THE TOFF
is his most engaging character.

IN CORONET BOOKS

ALSO BY JOHN CREASEY

VOTE FOR THE TOFF

Elections ought to be peaceful affairs—but when they go wrong it's useful to have a Toff in the offing

Those who know him, those who have shared his lifelong devotion to helping the under-dog, know that Rollison is not joking.

But there are others who think that his desire to contest a Parliamentary election is just a playboy's whim, a passing fancy . . . which is not so.

And still others who react with vicious threats and brutal murder because they think his politicking is just a cover for a foray against a ring of drug-pushers . . . which may be so.

World wide sales of John Creasey's books total over 65,000,000 copies.
THE TOFF
is his most engaging character.

IN CORONET BOOKS

THE WORLD-FAMOUS TOFF SERIES

BY JOHN CREASEY

IN CORONET BOOKS

All these books are available at your bookshop or newsagent, or can be ordered direct from the publisher. Just tick the titles you want and fill in the form below.

CORONET BOOKS, P.O. Box 11, Falmouth, Cornwall.

Please send cheque or postal order. No currency, and allow the following for postage and packing:

1 book—10p, 2 books—15p, 3 books—20p, 4–5 books—25p, 6–9 books—4p per copy, 10–15 books—2½p per copy, over 30 books free within the U.K.

Overseas—please allow 10p for the first book and 5p per copy for each additional book.

Name ....

Address ....

....